TO SAMARKAND AND BACK

BY

ROMA GELBLUM-BROSS

CORMORANT BOOKS

Published with the assistance of
The Canada Council and
The Ontario Arts Council.

Cover from a watercolour on paper
entitled *Bird's Spaces* by Judy Garfin,
courtesy of the artist
and The Canada Council Art Bank.

Typeset in Dunvegan by Greenglass Graphics.
Printed in Winnipeg by Hignell.

Published by Cormorant Books,
RR 1, Dunvegan, Ontario, K0C 1J0.

Canadian Cataloguing in Publication Data

Gelblum-Bross, Roma, 1937-
    To Samarkand and back

ISBN 0-920953-40-9

    1. World War, 1939-1945--Refugees--Fiction.
2. World War, 1939-1945--Poland--Fiction.
3. Samarkand (Uzbek S.S.R.)--Fiction. I. Title.

PS8563.E43T6 1988   C813'.54   C88-090252-3
PR9199.3.G44T6 1988

This collection of stories is dedicated, with affection and gratitude:

to my teacher, Terence Byrnes, for teaching me so much, for patience and effort above and beyond the call of duty;

to my analyst, Dr. Monroe Miller, for helping me to find myself;

and to my daughter, Amanda, for being the way she is.

CONTENTS

SHOES

The last thing my mother grabbed as we were hurriedly leaving our apartment in Kamenetz was a pair of fancy, high-heeled, black patent-leather shoes. She had almost forgotten them, but as we were standing in the door, she ran back, slid open the window of the glass cabinet where she had placed them, and brought them with her. She then untied the straps of the tightly packed knapsack and stuffed them in. At that moment Father gave her the kind of look he had for her whenever he thought she was doing something utterly silly. Mother saw this look, but said nothing. This was no time for arguments; even I who was only six could understand that. Father took me by the hand and the three of us went down the stairs, where a truck was waiting for us in the gray street to take us across the border and into Russia.

We came to Kamenetz from the town of Lodz, where we had lived before the war started. It was there Mother had ordered her shoes from Mr. Eleyahu Bendzik, a master shoemaker. She always ordered her shoes from Mr. Benzik, as did other women of our family. For the shoes he made were not only handsome, but also soft, light and strong.

Mr. Bendzik, so Mother told me, liked to "charge prices" for his shoes, for he had a large family and a wife who liked to "get dressed" and have good seats in the Synagogue during the High Holidays. But once you slipped Mr. Bendzik's shoes on your feet, so she said, you forgot the price, for his shoes gave one a foretaste of heaven, and this was not something that many shoemakers in Lodz could boast of.

So one day Mother decided she needed a pair of elegant shoes, the kind she could go dancing in. Since it was my Nanny's day off she decided to take me with her, and together we went to Yaracha street where the shoemaker had his workshop in the office of a large, yellowish building. When we arrived there, Mr. Bendzik was not in his best mood, for he had just accepted an order for high-heeled boots from a German officer on a visit to town. "They have a new fashion," he said, smirking. "Everybody wears shoes on high heels because Hitler is short."

When he heard Mother's request, his mood became even worse. "What do you need fancy shoes for?" he said. "To go dancing?" He shook his head sadly. "The way things are going, I am afraid we shall soon be dancing the dance of death, and for that dance one does not need any fancy shoes on high heels. So, if you want my advice, which nobody seems to want these days, as if all I could do was shoes, order yourself a pair of wings to fly, from my competition, across the street." There was a store across the street, where they molded angels and saints out of plaster for use in religious ceremonies and tombs.

"I do not like to order things that I do not need or that are not becoming, Mr. Bendzik," Mother answered, "therefore I cannot accept your suggestion. Please quote your price and make the shoes for me." She was not one who could be easily persuaded to give up the things she desired. She even agreed to pay the steep sum that the shoemaker had quoted, without haggling, as was the custom. Mr. Bendzik then told her to stand on a sheet of newspaper. He circled the outline of her feet on it with a thick pencil, the tip of which he had first put in his mouth. He wrote her name on the paper soles, then cut them with thick scissors and hung them on a metal hook that dangled above his head.

At dinner, when Father heard the price Mother was going to pay (which was smaller than the price that Mr. Bendzik had demanded), he raised a small storm and talked about his salary, which was not getting any bigger. But Mother took a package of good American cigarettes that she had bought for him on the way home out of her bag and the small storm passed. I remember the day when Mother came home with flushed cheeks and with a large white box in her hands. She summoned Nanny and our maid, Manya, to the bedroom, and I tagged along. She unwrapped the shoes carefully and placed one on the palm of her hand, as if it were a dainty figurine. She clicked her tongue and smiled, then put the shoes on.

The three of them stooped to admire the shoes. Then they all straightened their backs, and Mother stood in front of the long mirror and glanced at herself approvingly. The shoes made her look taller and also made her legs look much slimmer. She walked backwards and forwards in front of the mirror. Nanny and Manya clicked their tongues, and said: "Ho, Ho!" and "Look, look!" and other things.

Then we all moved to the living room, where Father was sitting enveloped in cigarette smoke. He looked at our small procession and shook his head, as if amazed at women's folly.

"So?" Mother said to him.

"So what?" Father answered. "Shoes are shoes, even if they come from Mr. Bendzik, who charges unreasonable prices."

I crawled nearer to where Mother was standing and examined the shoes. They were very nice shoes indeed. They were made of very shiny black leather which was slit in front to allow a triangle of soft gray suede to be inserted. They had a thin silver strap, and the heels had a silver metal inset. The soles were all new and pink and looked like large tongues. They squeaked a little when Mother walked, and the heels made a clicking sound on the floor.

Mother then told Manya to put them in the bedroom closet. Then the three of them left and I was there alone. I opened the door of the closet, took one of the shoes out and put it on my foot. It looked very funny and I quickly took it off and went back to my room.

On that night Mother and Father went out dancing, both looking very handsome. I heard the click, click of the shoes as Mother went down the stairs and then her happy laughter.

But that was the only time Mother wore the new shoes. One night, soon after she brought them home, we had to leave town.

9

I was told we were going on a long trip and that we were going to come back. By the light of a small lamp and very quietly, so as not to wake the maid, Mother and Father packed two large knapsacks, put some money and jewellery into small pouches that they hung on their necks and dressed me warmly. When the knapsack that she was packing was almost full, Mother took the shoes out of her closet. "Are you crazy?" Father said. "What are you taking these shoes with you for?" But Mother shrugged her shoulders. "They are brand new, and beautiful, almost a work of art, and I will go dancing in them yet." And she put the shoes in. Then the three of us tiptoed through the long dark corridor where I heard Manya's snoring, and I thougt how surprised she was going to be not to find us there in the morning.

When we came to Kamenetz, which was a pretty little town nestled in the midst of green mountains, and which, I was told, "was close to the border," though why it was important I did not know, we rented a furnished apartment. A glass-doored china cabinet stood in the living room, but since we had no china to put in it, Mother put in the shoes. They stood on the upper mahogany shelf, shiny and elegant looking.

Women who came to drink a cup of tea with Mother always asked her to take the shoes out, and they admired them loudly and enthusiastically. "Some shoes you have got there, Sophia Solomonovna, some shoes!" they said. The women smelled the leather, fingered it and admired its softness. They lifted the shoes on the palm of their hands and admired their evenness. They peeped inside to examine the finishing, and they declared that it was perfect. In short, they made much more fuss about them than I thought the shoes were worth: I thought the clicking of tongues and the "tsk, tsk," and the admiring looks were an exaggeration. But then these grown-up women had their ways and did and said things which I could not understand and which they told me were good and important, for they knew. I wished that I could be admitted into their secrets, but they hinted that I was too small to know everything and that I would know too when the time was ripe.

The truth of the matter was, though, that the shoes held some fascination for me too. When I was alone, I took them out of the cabinet. I liked the smell of the leather and its softness and the dark, deep shine. I liked to imagine Mr. Eleyahu Bendzik making them in his crowded workshop and sighing with pleasure when his work was done. I liked to imagine Mother dancing in the shoes and I liked to think that I too would once own them and go to dances in them, wearing a long dress and looking tall and pretty, like Cinderella at the ball. Sometimes I thought that those were, perhaps, magic shoes, like the red ones in Hans Christian Andersen's story, or the kind that could make wishes come true. Alone, at night, I was weaving stories of my own around the shoes, and the stories always had happy endings.

When we arrived in the town of Berdychev, in Russia, the shoes were still there in my mother's knapsack, though there were times when I thought we would have to part from them and from many other things that we had carried with us.

The truck in which the three of us had crossed the border broke very soon after, and we walked on strange frightening roads for many days and nights. At night, trees cast long shadows on the moonlit forest paths, and each shadow looked like a dark animal about to spring to life. Panting, large shapes moved around us, and sometimes rubbed against me. Carts drawn by horses came from behind and passed us, the drivers calling "Vio, horsie, Vio!" their whips cutting the air with a sharp swishing sound. Sometimes, a child cried plaintively, "aa, aaa," and was quickly silenced. I trudged along, held by Mother and Father. I was not used to walking such long distances; it was hard, but I had no choice. Twigs sometimes cut my face, and sometimes small stones rolled on my feet. No one talked.

Daylight came slowly and reluctantly. Foggy, damp mist lay on the yellow fields and on the gray roads. Then, when the sun finally rolled up heavily from behind the horizon, it was hot, and it scorched our faces. Poppies and cornflowers grew in great profusion in the wheat fields, and sunflowers, loaded with dark seeds bent their heads above hedges. Grinning peasants with bare feet stood on the sides of roads offering things to sell, to buy or to barter. "Shoes!" they cried. "Do you have any shoes for sale, or good shirts?" Sometimes, they stood mutely and watched us pass, their faces grim as if they were watching an unending funeral procession. When my legs were so weak I thought they would fold under me and I would fall, I cried to Father, and he

11

lifted me and carried me in his arms for a short while, till I rested a little; then he put me down again.

One night, when we were resting in the forest, we were attacked by a group of urchins who wanted to plunder our belongings. I heard sounds of heavy breathing and wrestling, then someone ran away with a yelp, cursing loudly. I was very frightened then, but I was too tired to be frightened very long and I fell asleep.

On the afternoon of our arrival in Berdychev, the town was calm and golden in the rays of the setting sun. Small houses with wooden porches lined the streets, and carts drawn by horses rattled on the cobblestones. People turned their heads to look at us and opened their eyes wide. A large woman wearing a kerchief asked, "You refugees? From Poland? Is it true what they say about Hitler? Is it that bad there?" When Father told her the Germans were close to the border, she laughed with disbelief and turned to go on her way.

We went to the city offices, where they gave us the name and address of a Jewish family that had a room for rent.

"A Mr. Lerer," they said, "and his two daughters. A decent man."

At the corner of Otvetzka Street, which was where we were heading, there was a ladies' wear store with a mirror and two mannequins in the window. The mannequins had glass eyes that stared blankly at us and they held their pink plaster palms outstretched as if asking for alms. They wore shapeless cotton dresses, their clumsy shoes were painted on the plaster, and their faces were cracked in a few places and unevenly painted over with dark, pink paint.

"Recent fashions, I see," Mother said and smiled, a little bitterly, I thought. I glanced in the mirror, which looked as if someone had spilled water over it and then had forgotten to wipe it off. Flies that kept beating against the window glass left it spotted with minute dots. In the midst of it all I saw myself, my father and mother reflected. At first I was not sure it was myself I was seeing there: I thought it was a strange girl, not at all the one I had last seen in Kamenetz trying the shoes on in front of the mirror. I too was a sloppy little mannequin, with a brown freckled face and clothes that hung like rags, my hair matted and dishevelled. I was covered with dust. I did not even look like a girl. I looked like a little hobo, like little Cinderella in the illustration of my book of fairy tales.

There was a hose in the garden of a corner house, the windows of which were bordered with plywood. We went into the garden. Mother washed her face and mine. The water felt nice on my parched skin. A refreshing gust of wind which came into the garden cooled my face and the leaves of the apple tree rustled. The wall of the house was red.

Mother said to Father: "Look, Father, a red sunset."

"It's the fires in Poland," Father answered, and they became quiet.

Number 33 was where we were to inquire. Father knocked and after a short while the door opened. I first saw a loud skirt with a design of squiggles, circles and squares. Then I raised my eyes and saw the woman who was wearing it. Her face was like that of a thin bird: narrow, dark and sharp featured. Her small, dark eyes, which were set in very deep sockets, peered at us inquiringly. "You from the city office?" She asked matter of factly. Father nodded. *"Zahodeetye!"* she said, "Come in!"

From the small hallway she took us to a darkish, empty corridor. I pulled on Father's hand. "Are we going to live here, Father? I don't like it here. When are we going to go back home?" But Father did not answer. Instead I heard the woman's voice.

"Papa!" she cried. "They came from the city office for the room. Refugees they sent us. Look at the shape they are in!"

Mother glanced at Father, who looked as if he had just emerged out of a stack of hay, and she combed her hair with her fingers. An old man then appeared in the door and started walking slowly towards us. He was bowlegged and was wearing pants on suspenders. His head was very round, and he wore round eyeglasses. The neatly trimmed gray beard somehow did not fit together with his bald head. There was some hair left just above his ears and he combed it back, so that it fell down and showed around his neck. His ears and his nose were hairy. Though he was not very wrinkled, he looked quite old. He came nearer, cleared his throat and looked up at Father.

"Lerer . . . is my name . . . greatly honored to have you, Mr. and Mrs. . . ." Father told him the name, "as guests in our house."

13

Then he stooped above me: "Ha, ha, you have a little girl too? Gone into the world like this? *Zhalko* ... pity ... My Irenochka and Clarochka used to be that small too once, but that was long, long ago." There was a faint smell of mothballs hanging around him, and his hand, which he lay on my head, was soft like a sponge.

Then the woman who had let us in spoke in a voice that reminded me of the squeak that an unoiled door hinge made.

"They look as if they came from a different world," she said, addressing her father. "Look at the kind of clothes they wear, and look at the shoes."

Mr. Lerer was embarrassed. He glanced pleadingly at his daughter, then said, "But Irenochka, *dushenka,* my little soul," and, looking at Father and Mother apologized to them. "It's the young generation, you know. No manners and no politeness." He then turned and motioned for us to follow him.

He brought us to a very small room in which there stood two metal cots with straw mattresses on them. He helped Mother undo her knapsack, then said, sighing, "The young now are filled with slogans the way that pillow is filled with feathers. Please feel at home here and join us for supper." He left then and closed the door behind him.

But the door opened again very soon, and it was as if a strong gust of wind had opened it, for it knocked against the wall with a loud thud. The red skirt flashed before my eyes again. It flashed before my eyes like a large flag flapping in the wind, then folded and fell around a pair of skinny, hairy legs in dark slippers. I looked up then and saw Irena's face again. She was smiling amicably, revealing a row of small sharp teeth, two of which protruded a little.

She came to introduce herself and her sister Clara, who came behind her. Clara had a brighter complexion and looked like a younger version of Mr. Lerer in a skirt. She ruffled my hair and her hand was like a sponge too.

Irena glanced around the room, and her eyes rested on our knapsacks. "Good, solid knapsacks," she said. "We do not have the likes of these in the Soviet Union." She touched the leather straps and examined the metal fittings curiously.

By that time, my mother had already opened her knapsack

14

and its contents lay spread on the cot. Irena eyed it all appreciatively. "Fancy goods!" she said. Then her eyes fell on the shoes. Her eyes were drawn to those two shining shoes as if they were magnets, and she stepped forward to the bed.

"You'll permit me, Sophia Solomonovna, to look at the shoes?" she said, a little more softly, as if the sight of them brought out all the femininity hidden beneath her rough exterior. She picked up the shoes and fingered the leather, then looked at the neatly formed heel. A strange expression appeared on her face, a mixture of attraction and repulsion, craving and contempt. "Some shoes," she said, "Some shoes." Her sister stood behind her and she too eyed the shoes with curiosity.

Then it looked as if something had snapped suddenly within Irena, for she cast Mother a contemptuous look and said, "Who needs shoes like these? Do you hope to go dancing here, in the Soviet Union with shoes like these? You'll be the laughing stock of the town wherever you go. We do not garb ourselves with such fancy stuff here. Shame, shame that people should occupy themselves with such nonsense!" She threw the shoes back on the bed; then, as if drawn by a magnet, she picked them up again.

"You would not mind, Sophia Solomonovna, if I tried them on just for fun, ah?" Mother shook her head. "No, why, go ahead, Irena Borisovna."

Irena sat on the cot and slipped her hairy feet into Mother's dainty shoes. The shoes were a little narrow for her, but she finally got them on and went out to the corridor to look at herself in the mirror. I followed her and peeped at her from the entrance to the room. She looked taller and slimmer wearing the shoes, and her flowing skirt looked more elegant when she stood there wearing them. She must have noticed the change in her appearance too, for she stood in front of the mirror for a long time and turned around to see her back. Her sister smacked her lips and said, *"Kak krasivo!"*

Irena took the shoes off with a grimace and brought them back to the room. Clara stayed behind, in the corridor.

"Ridiculous stuff, vestige of bourgeois life!" she said, and threw the shoes on the bed. She then left the room, slamming the door behind her.

"Throw the shoes out, they are only trouble," Father said.

15

"You won't need them here for a while." And he glanced around at the empty room.

"I see no reason why I should throw perfectly good shoes out just because I cannot use them for a while," Mother answered, and the reason behind her answer must have had its effect on Father, for he only said, "Well, when I married you, I knew there were some '*meshugenes*' in your family."

"And in yours," Mother retorted.

I smiled for the first time since we entered this gloomy house. I liked it when Mother and Father bickered about their families, for bickering made them say funny things which were not true. The swarm of aunts, uncles and cousins, a few of whom always seemed to be visiting or just dropping by, were pleasant and funny people who smiled and gossiped a lot and kidded each other with jokes and nicknames. They held me on their knees and tickled me under the chin and talked to me softly and affectionately and brought me presents and toys. The mention of them filled this cold, strange room with warmth. My grandfather Naftaly appeared in my memory too and then my grand aunt Rivkeh. She stared at me from above her large bosom which was swathed in a silk fitted dress, her eyes narrowing with pleasure as she smiled at me.

There was a loud knock on the door. "*Uzhyn!*" announced Irena's scratchy voice summoning us to the dining room.

Mother took out of her knapsack the bread and sausage that we had bought from a farmer on the road. Out of a small cotton pouch that was attached to her belt, she took a few pinches of tea leaves and a few sugar cubes, and she put them on a piece of newspaper which she let me carry. Father took his pouch of tobacco leaves. Then we crossed the corridor and entered the dining room.

Irena and Clara were already there setting the table. They lay on it an untrimmed piece of white cloth, on top of which they placed a few bowls and cutlery that had handles of wood. Mother placed the food she had bought on the table. Irena and Clara eyed it greedily and both smiled sweetly.

"But Mrs. Solomonovna, really, you are too generous."

Irena took the sausage off the table and sniffed at it hungrily, then cut herself a piece from the end. "*Vkusnoye!*" she said,

"Tasty!" and she looked at us more kindly.

Then Mr. Lerer entered the room and sat at the head of the table, across from Father and with his back to the large window that faced the street. His entrance made the room feel more pleasant, for he slightly resembled my grandfather Naftaly, whom I loved. He said a few words to my father, and I looked around the room. This room too had very little furniture, and its walls were white and empty, except for a large portrait of a man with a black moustache and many medals on his chest. Across from it, on the opposiste wall, hung an old clock encased in a wood-and-glass cabinet. Its two thin, wiry arms looked as if they were trying to squeeze the number six, which had a protruding round belly and bent head. The brass gong swayed back and forth unmindful of what was going on above, and produced the rhythmic tic-toc which I liked to listen to.

Clara brought the soup in an aluminum pot and ladled it into the bowls. It was a yellow soup on the surface of which floated kernels of corn. It tasted terrible, but Mother forced me to eat it. Clara and Irena regarded Mother carefully as she ate. They tried to imitate the way Mother held her knife and fork, but they could not. Then Mother cut the sausage into pieces and put it on slices of black bread. Then they started talking.

"You from a big city?" asked Irena.

"Yes, Lodz, manufacturing city, textiles . . . "

"And you, what were you, a manufacturer or a worker?" Irena asked, looking at Father sharply.

"Both," Father answered smilingly. "I worked for my father, who used to own a factory."

Irena's eyes glistened. She clenched her fist.

"A capitalist, eh?" she said. "An exploiter of human labor!"

There was a zeal and an energy in her tone that frightened me, and I shrivelled inside.

Father was taken aback, but he answered her calmly.

"Not really, Miss Borisovna," he said. "My father and I worked very hard in that factory. It was a difficult and unpleasant trade. There were only a small number of people working in that plant, and they all loved and respected my father, who is an upright man."

Irena was not satisfied. Her eyes were suspicious and angry

17

and her brown little fists lay on the table clenched.

"How many rooms did you people live in?"

"Five."

"For three people?"

"Yes, there was also a maid and a nanny."

Irena looked at my parents through narrowed eyes.

"That's exactly what I thought! Maid, nanny, five rooms, what else?"

Old Mr. Lerer buried his face in his hands.

"But Irenochka, dear, *dushenka,* my little soul," he said soflty. "*Pozhaluysta,* please calm down. Look at these poor people. All this is past. Now they have nothing but what they carry on their backs . . . less than you and I . . . They are our guests, you know, Jews, like us. Where is your sense of the old Russian hospitality?"

"It's dead and buried, Father, together with old Russia."

"My God, Irenochka, but . . . "

"You and your God, Papa, you and your useless old God. We are also finished with God in the Soviet Union."

The old man smiled wistfully. "But I am not sure God is finished with us." And he turned to look through the window into the red street. The window of the house that stood across the street looked as if it were ablaze. Mr. Lerer's eyes went to the old clock, the wiry arms of which were courting the number seven. His eyes then moved to the man with the moustache.

"*Eto tak,*" he said to Father and looked at him as if he were searching in his eyes for understanding. "This is how things are. All this is easy for them," and he pointed to his daughters, "for they believe. But I . . . I am a divided man, divided many times. I do not know whether there is much of a man left." He said it with much feeling, and they were all silent after that. Then as if waking from sleep Mr. Lerer said, very quickly, "Let's stop this talk now. You must be tired and in need of rest. Clara, bring the samovar in!"

Clara went out and returned carrying the samovar. It was an old silver samovar, stately and shiny, decorated with embossed leaves and curls. A small teapot sat squatting on the top and in the slots at the bottom glistened dark red coals. Clara placed the samovar in the middle of the table. My face stared at me from the samovar all stretched and rounded. My parents were there too, with small bodies, flat noses and big ears. The man with the moustache and the clock were there, flowing and shapeless, as if they were to dissolve any minute. I asked permission to get up, and I went to the other side of the table, from where I could see the reflection of Mr. Lerer and his two daughters in the samovar. They too were distorted and funny, but on that side the samovar was red, for it reflected the blazing window's glare. I became flowing and red too, and then I went to the other side of the table, and I became white again.

Mr. Lerer started showing some marks on the samovar to my parents, and they inquired after its make and its age, while Clara poured tea into the glasses. The aroma of strong tea filled the room, and the samovar gave out pleasant warmth. Mother gave me a cube of sugar to suck on and poured some strong amber-colored essence into my glass. Mr. Lerer leaned back in his chair and sang a familiar Jewish tune.

> *Enlightened lords and sages,*
> *Do tell us how,*
> *The Emperor drinks tea.*
> *You don't know?*
> *Well, then I'll tell you:*
> *They take a big lump of sugar,*
> *Bore a hole in it,*
> *Then fill it with the boiling infusion,*
> *And stir it up . . .*
> *The sweet liquor*
> *They hand over*
> *To the Emperor!*

After having finished singing, Mr. Lerer cupped his hands around the tea glass, then gulped it with enjoyment. "Aaaa . . ." he said. The tension in his voice was gone, and he resembled my grandfather Naftaly, who also said "Aaaa . . ." and patted himself on the belly when he drank his afterdinner tea. My aunts Tonya and Dora asked him then, "Another glass of tea, Papa?" and he would answer, "A man is not a barrel . . . But on second thought, maybe it's not such a bad idea. But make it strong and with a slice of lemon."

My memories were interrupted by Irena's sharp voice. "This girl should be asleep now instead of gazing into samovars," she said. Her voice scratched my ear like a grater. I did not want to go to sleep alone in the small dark room. But Mother's voice came quiet and subdued, "Of course, Irena Borisovna, you are absolutely right, we shall put her to bed at once."

Father carried me to the other room.

I lay on the straw mattress in my clothes, the way I had always gone to sleep ever since we left Kamenetz. I stared into the darkness and was afraid. I could hear the voices in the other room, but could not hear what it was they were talking about. The memory of my grandfather Naftaly left a small sharp anguish around my heart. I tried to rub it away with my fingers, but it refused to be rubbed off. The sharp straws that pierced the mattress-cover pricked my hands and feet. My parents came in and started whispering. I twisted and turned and yawned. I did not like being here, I was more afraid here than out in the forest. I was wondering when our trip was going to come to an end. Towards the morning, when the little window of the room was turning gray, I fell asleep.

I did not sleep long, and woke up to the sound of many voices. When I sat up on my bed I saw headlike shapes outlined in the shadow of the window-frame that lay on the bright floor. I turned towards the window and saw the heads. There were many of them, one on top of the other, and they peered at me with many dark eyes. There were noses and cheeks flattened against the glass and yellow teeth with gaps in between. There were also stubby, dirty fingers in that window, and the fingers were pointing at me.

"Father!" I cried.

But the bed next to mine was empty. There were many voices coming from the other room. I got off the cot and crossed the corridor. I saw my parents standing in the middle of the dining room. Clara and Irena were sitting at the table and so were a few men dressed in uniforms. Black revolvers were attached to the men's belts and they smoked cigarettes, the butts of which they threw on the floor. At the head of the table sat a man in a rounded cap who wore ribbons of many colours on his chest and had shiny buttons on his uniform. The man was writing something with a pen which he dipped in an inkwell, pressing his chin against the thick, red throat.

"Good Russian you speak, citizen. How is that?" he addressed Father.

"I learned it in school," Father answered.

"You speak German too?"

Father shook his head. The man laughed into his chin.

"Of course you won't admit it, smart Jewish devil that you are, even if you spoke German better than ten Hitlers."

Loud laughter followed his words and the man looked pleased with his own smartness.

"Father!" I cried.

He looked at me surprised, as if he did not expect to see me there, then he pressed his finger against his lips. Irena got up and led me to the corner, where I remained standing behind the fat man in the round cap. He went on asking questions and then wrote the answers down in his large notebook with checkered pages. He had a boat-shaped ink-blotter which he used whenever the ink splattered on the page. Everybody around watched respectfully, and the people whose faces were glued to the window ceased their noise. The room became very bright and quiet then, and almost cheerful, like on the day of my auntie Tonya's wedding. She and her husband Morris stood in the middle of the room, the way Mother and Father were standing now, and the Rabbi sat at the table, though he did not have a blotter. A scribe was scribbling things down with a quill pen, his white beard shaking and his skullcap slipping off his head. Soon, the procession will go out, I shall hold the bride's veil and the people outside will cheer and throw confetti at us.

Instead, the door was darkened by a figure that lay a quivering, dark shadow on the sunlit floor. The figure saluted the man in the cap and handed a sealed letter to him. The man read it briefly, then quickly got up and ordered the soldiers to take Mother and Father out; one of them came to me and took me by the hand and the others surrounded Mother and Father. Then we all went outside, where the sun was already high up. There was quite a crowd assembled around the house. They parted before us. They stretched their necks, pointed to us with their fingers, laughed maliciously and whispered between them.

"*Shpyony*," they said, "*Nemetskeye shpyony*."

Though I did not know they were calling us spies then, I knew that what I heard had a sharp and malignant sound, and that it was directed at us. It made me shiver inside. When we stopped at the gate, a voice behind me said, "Could you believe it, batyushka, that they would take such a small girl in tow?"

A male voice answered, "Sure, don't you know, the cunning bastards are capable of anything. Don't forget it's war time. It's for the purpose of camouflage. I know something in these matters."

The first voice sighed and said, "*Bozhe, bozhe,* God, God, just look what people have come to in this world, look what people are capable of."

The male voice said, "*Da, da,*" and sighed too.

I looked around me. I could not understand it at all. It was only a few hours ago that we were sitting at the table with the samovar, Mr. Lerer singing pleasantly and talking politely to my parents, and all of a sudden we were surrounded by these soldiers with grave faces who were taking us to some place where we did not want to go. My hand felt so small and helpless inside the rough, warm hand of the soldier, whose face was hovering somewhere high above me underneath the metal helmet.

"*Dziadzia!*" I pulled on his hand. "Uncle, where are you taking us?"

"To the police station, to be tried."

"What does 'tried' mean, uncle?"

"Wait and see," he said.

A small truck arrived at the gate and I was hauled into it. Then Mother and Father were ordered to climb up, and they did. The soldiers climbed in after them and sat on the bench. The man in the round cap climbed into another car. Then the truck was jumping and rattling on the cobblestones. I could see the street, bordered by the frame of the truck receding fast. The town did not look the way it had looked on the previous evening, when it was calm and warm. The glare of the sun was hard and bright and the shadows of the trees that lined the streets were very black and solid. People had dark solid shadows attached to them too, and they too seemed to recede from us fast. The canvas became hot above our heads, and the soldier wiped the sweat off his brows with his sleeve. Then the buildings became sparcer, and in the spaces between them I saw again the yellow undulating fields spotted with the red of poppies and the deep, vibrant blue of the cornflowers. A fresh, hot smell wafted from the fields. Mother breathed in deeply, then breathed out again.

The truck stopped with a thud in front of a whitewashed building surrounded by a barbed wire fence. A sentry opened a wire gate, and the truck rolled in. Soldiers and policemen stood at the narrow entrance smoking cigarettes and clearing their throats noisily, then spitting on the ground. Their shadows too were harsh and dark, and the points of their bayonets were sharp and long. The asphalt of the surrounding yard burned and glittered like glass.

A soldier lifted me with one arm and stepped off the truck with me, holding me as if I were a bundle. He saluted another soldier in a round hat who stood in the entrance.

"And what is this?" the soldier asked, pointing to me. He had nice gray eyes and bright hair that showed from beneath the severe cap.

"*Shpyony!*" answered the soldier who was carrying me.

The officer looked at me, then at Father and Mother in disbelief, then spat and shook his head. "Either I am crazy, or the whole world is," he said with a grimace. He walked away shaking his head, and then he disappeared around the corner.

The place we were brought into was a long, dark, corridor with nothing but two benches that were placed against the wall. Nobody occupied these benches. The sentry instructed us to sit at the farthest end, where the two walls met the third, narrow one. Mother, Father and I sat there in a row, and I noticed that there were doors in the wall opposite the one where we sat. The first had a small glass window. The three other doors were of solid wood. The light from the outside made a square reflection in the dark corridor. Silhouettes of people appeared and disappeared from the square like figures in a shadow theatre. Father put his hand on top of mine and said, "Don't be afraid, I am here." I snuggled up to him.

"I flushed it down the toilet," Mother whispered to Father.

"You flushed what down?"

"The passport, with the German visa."

"Thanks heaven," Father said. "But don't talk, walls have ears, you know."

"What are they going to do to us?" Mother whispered.

"I hope it's not going to be the worst," Father replied.

A small, cold fear stole into my heart. I buried my face in Father's chest and listened to the rhythmic thud thud of his heart.

One of the doors opened then, and a large woman in a uniform came out. She was followed by an officer in high boots. She laughed loudly at what he said, lifting one of her shoulders slightly and shaking her blond hair, which was arranged in long ringlets. As soon as the officer left, the smile was gone from the woman's face and she turned around and stared at us coldly and severely. "You stay where you are," she instructed Father curtly. "And you," she pointed to Mother and me, "you follow me."

I was afraid of this large red-faced woman with the yellow hair, and I grabbed Mother's hand. It was cold and sweaty. The large woman opened a dark door with a key and ordered us to go in.

The room we entered was white and had no windows. I had never seen a room with no windows. A bare bulb dangled from a black wire that was tied in a loop. Beneath it stood a table made of unfinished wood. The only other item in the room was an aluminum basin, filled with water, which was placed on a low stool clumsily constructed from pieces of wood.

The woman ordered Mother and me to undress. I did not want to undress in front of her, and I made a gesture of refusal. But Mother looked at me sternly, and I knew I had to do as the woman had ordered. I put my clothes in a pile on the cement floor and stood there shivering, though it was not cold in the room. Mother undressed too. It was the first time I had ever seen my mother all naked, and I watched her curiously. I noticed with surprise how big her breasts were when she took off her brassiere and how heavy and veined her legs. She also had a patch of dark hair below her belly, where I did not have any hair. The sight of my mother naked made me forget my fear.

The woman picked the clothes off the floor and examined them one by one. She took out of the pocket of my jacket an old

24

candy wrapper that had a funny picture on it and looked at it closely. Then she smoothed it out by pressing it with her fingernail, and left it on the table. Then she looked over Mother's clothes, tore the buttons off and ripped the seams of her jacket. She also tore the shoulder pillows and emptied them of the gray stuffing. Dust came out of them in small puffs and the woman sneezed. She then threw Mother's clothes in one heap on the floor and pushed the pile away with her foot. She wore heavy shoes with square heels. She told me to stand in the corner, then turned away and stood facing the tall table in the middle of the room. From where I was, I could see her broad back, the ringlets that dangled from her head, and the crooked seams of her stockings.

"Climb on top of this table and lie on your back!" she ordered Mother.

Mother approached slowly. She had goose pimples over her skin and looked like a plucked chicken. The table was high, and the woman helped Mother by placing her hands under Mother's buttocks and hoisting her up. Mother lay on the table quietly.

"Spread your legs!" the woman ordered harshly, and I saw Mother's feet emerging from both sides of the woman's body.

Then I saw the woman's hand thrust forward and move jerkily back and forth. Mother screamed. I felt paralyzed. "Shut up!" yelled the woman. I wanted to cry and run for help, but the door was locked, and I was afraid. Then the woman told Mother to lie on her stomach, and when Mother was turning over, I saw her face for a brief moment. She did not look like my mother at all. Her face was red and puffed, her eyes were wide open and with no expression in them and her hair fell in limp strands from her sweaty forehead. She seemed to be looking at me, but not seeing me.

Mother turned to lie on her stomach, and I saw the woman spreading her buttocks with her hand. Then she stretched out a finger of the other hand and put it into Mother. Mother screamed again and the scream was sharp and piercing and sent shivers down my spine. The woman took her finger out of Mother and rinsed her hand in the basin of water. I saw her face then and it was contorted in a terrible grimace. The water turned yellow, and it stank terribly in the room.

I pressed my nose with my fingers. I started crying. "Shut up! Shut up!" cried the woman. "If you won't stop crying, I'll lock you in a cell!" She came to me and covered my mouth with her stinking hand. I saw Mother slowly getting off the table, holding her hand on the patch of hair. The woman threw her a malevolent look, then leaned forwards and peered at me. "It's your turn, little girl." She hoisted me up then and before I knew what was happening to me, I was laid on the table on my back, and the woman's hand was pressing against my belly. Her other hand held my legs down.

"Spare the child, we are not spies, she has nothing hidden inside her!" Mother cried. I turned and saw her standing there shivering, the veins of her legs purple and swollen and her breasts hanging down sadly.

"*Moltchy!*" the woman yelled again. "It's we who decide what needs to be done and what does not need to be done!"

Then I felt her spreading my legs and I felt her finger and fingernail inside me. It hurt terribly and I screamed. She put her other hand, still stinking, on my mouth. I was suffocating. I could not breathe. I felt her finger getting deeper and deeper. She was poking and scratching me all inside, going deeper and deeper in. She leaned above me, and I saw her red face and her yellow teeth. There were beads of sweat on her forehead. It was as if the whole weight of her large body was on top of me. I wanted to scream but I could not. I wanted to get out, to run away, but I was held by her hands like by a vice. Something was pressing on my chest, something was pressing on me from inside as if it wanted to tear me apart. It hurt terribly, as if something burst inside me, and I screamed and saw a large darkness and in the darkness I did not see the big woman and the white room anymore.

I came to slowly and painfully. It seemed to me I was emerging out of some cold darkness which was turning into a gray, painful haze. The yellowish, shivering wires of the electric bulb above my head were what I saw first, and then I saw Father's black face and eyes above me. Father's face was wet. "I want to go home, Father!" I cried. "I want to go home." But he only said, "Tsh, be quiet, be quiet, it's all over, it's all over."

26

Mother was above me too. Her face was black, and she was wearing her torn jacket hanging loosely on her shoulders, like on a scarecrow. At the end of the corridor, the cigarette that the sentry was smoking glowed in the dark, and mosquitoes and little flies circled the bulb feverishly and frantically. Mother put a scarf around my neck. "Here, sleep now," she said.

I tried to sleep, but could not. Waves of heat and cold came over me, and the tip of the sentry's cigarette was like a large, red firefly. The doors stood dark and threatening, and the gray walls seemed to be closing around me. Father and Mother's faces hung above me motionless. Father's mouth was open, as if he was crying to someone in his sleep, and his belly made squeaky noises. When the entrance to the corridor became gray, soldiers and policemen began walking in and disappearing behind the dark doors. Then I fell asleep.

I woke to the sound of loud cries. Two men were being pushed from behind through the entrance, their hands raised to their heads. *"Nein!"* they cried in Yiddish. *"Nein,* we are not spies!" A soldier prodded them into the first room. I stared at it all frightened, still aching all over. Mother and Father were frightened too and their lips were pale. The two men, who wore skullcaps on their curly black hair, emerged from the first room and were led to the room where I and Mother had been. When they went in there, I closed my eyes. I expected to hear screams, but it was silent in that room. They were there for a short while only. The door jerked open, and they came out wearing kerchiefs over their eyes. Two soldiers with bayonets followed them, and an officer in a round cap. The young men screamed and resisted. "It's all a misunderstanding, *tovarishchi!"* they cried. "The Gilettes were bought in Poland, not in Germany!" But nobody listened. They were led out, and more soldiers with bayonets came out of the rooms. The police station became very quiet and the skin on Mother and Father's face looked tight, as if it had been stretched over their bones and dried. Then, there was a very faint noise, like that of firecrackers, in the distance. At the sound of this noise my parents' heads fell down, and I saw that they were crying.

When the soldiers started filing back in, I noticed that outside the sun was up. The small square of sky that showed

27

through the opening was filled with curly, frivolous clouds which looked like little puffs of cotton that someone had scattered there quite thoughtlessly. The corridor looked more cheerful, and the sentry was drinking coffee from a large mug. I got off Father's lap and sat on the bench staring out. The sentry finished drinking his coffee, got up and went to the front room. He emerged carrying a few slices of black bread and steaming tea in a metal jug, which he brought to us. I ate hungrily and drank the strong, sweet tea from an aluminum cup.

The bells started ringing somewhere in the distance. "It's Sunday," Father said. The sound of these bells reverberated within me and brought with it the memory of Nanny, who took me to church with her every Sunday. We walked under golden chestnut trees and the yellow-red leaves rustled under our feet. I collected the brown, smooth chestnuts and put them in my pockets. Girls in white dresses wearing white wreaths hurried past us on their way to the first communion looking pretty, like little brides. In the church, there was a splendid altar, the choir sang beautifully and on the way back the bells sang their melodies till we came home.

But as I listened to the bells ringing, I knew all of a sudden and with a pang of pain and fear inside, that all this was gone and that the trip I was on was not a real trip at all. I knew suddenly and clearly that I might not see my Nanny again for a very long time, and that a very long time would pass before we returned. I did not feel like the same girl who had walked with Nanny under the chestnut trees. Something had changed within me, something was heavy and dull in me, and there was an aching emptiness inside that had not been there before. I wanted to cry out to my parents and ask them why they had cheated me, but their faces were tired, sad and distant, and I did not.

Suddenly, the sky became overcast. The sentry ran in cursing, then came back wearing a dark, shiny cape. It started raining, and it became very dark. Then thunder started rolling, one roll coming in the wake of the other, and it was as if hundreds of empty barrels rolled off a mountain. I curled up to Father, whose hand was cold. The little building shook and drops of rain rattled on the metal roof. It sounded as if the whole world was engaged in a furious battle with itself.

Then, as suddenly, it became very still again, and I could hear the sounds of drops falling off the roof on the gravel path outside, and the plop plop of water running into the sewers. I closed my eyes. When I opened them again, I was staring into the face of the blond woman leaning above me. I screamed and felt a hand over my mouth. I thought I would hear her voice again, but it was the voice of my Father, calm and warm, telling me it was all over, all over, again. But I felt the hands of the woman on me and inside me, and it was as if she had left part of herself in me.

I fell asleep in my father's lap then, but it was a heavy sleep interrupted by nightmares. I woke up frequently, and Father calmed me and wiped the sweat off my face. I screamed like the young men in the kerchiefs, *"Nein! Nein!"* but no one was listening to me.

Then it was morning again, and Father was putting the rim of a warm metal cup to my lips. I gulped the sweet tea. Its warmth and sweetness gave me a pleasant feeling that drowned a little of the pain that I held inside. "Drink, drink!" urged Father's voice, and I drank one cup after another till my belly felt full. Then I sat on the bench and ate a piece of bread.

There was much movement in the corridor, people rushed in and out, it was a regular business day. "What's going to happen to us? When are we going to be tried?" Father asked a passing policeman, but the policeman just shrugged his shoulders and said, "They will let you know."

With all the people coming in and out, it was more cheerful at the police station. I stared at the big moustaches of the men, at the shiny badges and the uniforms. Some civilians sat in the corridor now, and they smiled at us, as if surprised to see me there. Mother combed my hair and buttoned my little sweater.

Then I heard a sound of arguing voices out in the yard. Someone was demanding entry, arguing loudly with the sentry. The older male voice had a familiar sound, though whose it was I could not recall.

"You must have a pass, a permission to enter!" insisted a young voice.

"But I must enter, talk to your commandant, it is a matter of urgency," said the older.

There was a flurry of movement close to the door. A soldier

entered the office behind the door with the window, then emerged holding a piece of paper in his hand. A few minutes later he reappeared and behind him, to our surprise, we saw Mr. Lerer, his hair dishevelled and his clothes in some disarray.

"Mr. Lerer!" Father cried. Is it possible, you too!" But Mr. Lerer had already disappeared behind the door. He was carrying a small parcel with him.

"I wonder why Mr. Lerer is here," Father said to Mother.

"Perhaps he has brought us some food," Mother answered.

After a while, Mr. Lerer reentered the corridor, and behind him the thick-necked official in the round cap walked slowly. He was shaking his head, then nodding sadly. "Women, women," I heard him say. "I shall never understand them as long as I live." Then both started walking towards us. Although it was quite dark in the corridor, I could see that Mr. Lerer's face was sad and that his eyes were red. He approached us with his head hanging down, and he put his soft spongy hand on my head.

"Are you all right, sweet girl, feeling fine?" he asked leaning towards me and looking at my face. I shook my head and sobbingly hid it in Father's pants.

"You are free, you can leave!" I heard the fat officer's voice. "There is not going to be any trial."

I turned around, surprised and happy, and saw him standing and looking at me with a wide smile. "Yes, little girl, you can leave!"

My mother jumped off the bench and kissed the official's hand impulsively. "*Spaseebo, bolshoyeh spaseebo!* Thank you, commandant!" she cried. There was a wide, though pained and unbelieving smile on Father's face. He too stood up and was shaking the officer's hand very warmly. Then he took the pouch of tobacco that he was carrying with him off his belt and handed it to the policeman.

"Please, accept it, with my gratitude!

"I'll take the tobacco, thank you, I cannot refuse that, but you owe your thanks to citizen Lerer here. Without his intervention . . . " He raised his hand up in a fleeting motion. " . . . I do not know what would have happened. Thank him!"

Father and Mother looked at Mr. Lerer with gratitude, but he just stood there with his head bowed and avoided their eyes. He

30

held the small parcel that he had brought with him to his chest and mumbled something to himself. Mother opened her mouth as if she wanted to say something to him, but just then a soldier came out of the office carrying our knapsacks in his hands. Mr. Lerer took one, Father took the other. Mother took me by the hand, and we quickly went out through the door and the iron gate. The sun shone brightly, and there was no trace of yesterday's storm. The city was as calm as if nothing had ever happened, as if what had gone on in that white building was only a nightmare. Already, the carts were rattling on the cobblestones, and people were lining up in front of the bakery across the street. The top leaves of the trees began to rustle, and little by little the rustling current worked its way down to the lower branches. Unaccustomed to such brightness, we stood there squinting.

Mr. Lerer handed the brown parcel to Mother.

"Accursed shoes," he said. "Throw them away."

Mother, surprised, unwrapped the package. Her black shoes were in it, their metal-studded heels shining in the sun.

"What?" she said with astonishment. "The shoes were left in your house? They were not in our knapsacks when the policeman brought them along? And you brought them now? At a time like this. . . ? You remembered. But this is incredible, I do not know how to thank you."

Mr. Lerer stared at her with his sad, pained eyes.

"What?" he said. "So you suspected nothing? You knew nothing?"

Mother looked at him with a deep questioning frown. Then she shook her head as if she wanted to shake off the thoughts and the suspicion that had gathered there.

"No, Mr. Lerer. I . . . I do not understand . . . What is it that you mean?"

Then her head jerked as if shaken by a sudden flash of understanding. She stared at Mr. Lerer, and her lips quivered. Then she said, her eyes narrowing and her lips pursed:

"What? Is that possible at all? Irena? She. . . ? My dear God, but that's unbelievable . . . "

Mr. Lerer's eyes filled with tears. His lips quivered too, and he shuffled his feet looking shaken, confused and ashamed. I remembered him singing jocularly at the table and was sorry to

31

see him so broken. He bowed his head again and muttered, almost inaudibly, *"Izvenyete,* forgive us, if you can, forgive Irena ... The devil only knows ... Things seem to fall apart ... " and he clasped Mother's hand in his and leaned forward to kiss it. *"Izveneyte, pozhaluysta ... "*

He turned away from us quickly, as if he could not stand being there any longer and started walking in a fast pace towards the wide shady street that opened into the square.

I watched him go with sorrow. I was so happy about his reappearance and about our sudden release. I could still feel the soft touch of his spongy hand on my head, and already he was going away, mournful and upset. It was as if grandfather Naftaly were leaving us for the second time. The first time was when grandfather had parted from us at the train station of Lodz. When he said farewell and so long there had been such unspeakable, deep sadness in his eyes that I started crying. His beard shook as he was waving to us. When Father cried, "See you, Papa!" grandfather pointed to the sky.

Mother and Father must have felt like me, for they too looked after Mr. Lerer with expressions of great sadness.

It was the first time since we had exited the dim police station that I clearly saw my parents' faces. They seemed different from the way they had been a few days ago, at the Lerer's dinner table. Father's face was sallow and unshaven, and his eyes were framed in deep bluish shadows. On Mother's face a thin net of wrinkles seemed to have formed overnight. As they looked at each other, there was strangeness and embarrassment in their eyes and much fatigue.

"So, it was Irena ... " Mother said and nodded sadly, then moved her hand as if she wanted to chase the thought away.

"I suspected her," Father answered, "though I thought it was for a different reason ... ideology and all that ... How fortunate that Mr. Lerer is a man with a conscience."

"And with a heart," Mother added.

She kept turning the shoes in her hands as if not knowing what to do with them. I looked at them too and all of a sudden I thought I *knew*, like the women in Kamenetz. There was a secret about these shoes that we all shared, and I was now in the secret too. I did not understand it all, but I now knew that they were magic shoes after all. Irena must have known too, and she desired them; she wanted to take them away from us. I almost jumped with joy. I wanted to share my discovery with my parents, but I did not know the right words and was afraid they wouldn't understand. So I kept it a secret and I peeped at the shoes curiously to see whether they had changed in any way.

The bakery across the street had just opened, and there were more people passing us by and staring at us curiously. Father gathered the straps of his knapsack.

"Mr. Lerer told you to throw the shoes away," he said to Mother. "So why don't you throw them away?"

I looked at Mother. I knew she wouldn't throw them away and I did not want her to. She pursed her lips and, leaning above the knapsack, opened the side pockets and pushed the shoes in.

"I'm going to dance in these shoes, I'm telling you, when it's all over, I'm going to dance."

"Yes, when it's all over I'm going to dance!" I repeated after her. My voice sounded to me thicker and so serious. Father looked at us and made a motion of acceptance or resignation with his hand. He helped Mother to hoist the knapsack on her back and asked a passerby for directions. Then he took me by the hand, and we turned towards the road that led to Kiev.

THE BLACK VALISES

I first noticed Robert Engel on the platform of the old Kiev Station. Mother, Father and I were waiting for a train to take us into Russia and away from the German front. What caught my attention were his valises.

The station was densely crowded with refugees, who carried their belongings in knapsacks, bundles and old valises bursting open at the seams. Only Robert Engel had large new valises. They were black and shiny, had gold coloured locks and were braced with wide bands of metal. Robert Engel himself looked small and insignificant next to his valises; he was very skinny, had red, thinning hair and a thin, pale nose that supported a pair of gold-rimmed glasses.

He was standing not far from us on the platform. When the train finally rolled into the station and people crowded the entrance pushing and screaming, Father helped Engel up the steep metal steps.

But after we had boarded the train we lost sight of him. He was pushed to the left of the long dim carriage. We were pushed to the right. We settled quickly on one of the still-vacant benches. Even before Father had taken off his coat I fell asleep on his shoulder.

When I woke up early in the morning the train was moving slowly and heavily. It was emitting gasping, forced sounds which were interrupted from time to time by the long wailing cry of the whistle. The bolts underneath the carriage squeaked shrilly with every turn and the wagon shook and rattled. Chilly misty air shrouded the windows. Shadows of telegraph poles were moving hastily on the panes, and frost clung in uneven patches to the greenish-gray metal of the window frame. The leg of someone seated on the roof of the wagon dangled in front of our window.

When my eyes got used to the semi-darkness I saw human shapes that crouched, sat or lay on benches, on the floor, and on the luggage racks. They all looked as if they had just given up a night-long struggle with sleeplessness and had frozen into twisted positions, their hands clutching their belongings. Children were crying in their sleep. Enamelled nightpots attached to the bundles gave off a smell of urine that mingled with the smoke of handmade cigarettes, the sweat of dozens of unwashed bodies and the odour of rotting food. My parents' heads were moving silently back and forth, like the heads of marionettes forgotten by their puppeteer. It was stuffy, cold and deadly quiet.

The silence was interrupted by the metallic squeak of an opening door. When the door closed again I saw a man in a khaki uniform with Russian emblems, standing in the entrance. He squinted, then looked around in astonishment. With the tip of his boot he nudged one of the bodies blocking the passage.

"Move a little, batyushka, allow a fellow to perform his duty, ah?" he said loudly. He spoke Russian and the tone of his voice was deep, warm and melodious. Eyes opened and some faces lit up with smiles.

"Some aromatic stuff in this wagon, comrades," he went on. How about opening a window or two. Mother Russia has plenty of fresh air, if nothing else. So go ahead and enjoy it."

He stretched a leg over a body that was curled up between two crowded seats and pushed one of the windows outward. Fresh cold air burst into the wagon, bringing with it minute particles of ice that melted on faces and beards. People shrank back, pulled on the edges of shawls and coats. Mother woke up with a shiver and wrapped me in her blanket. The official reached the middle of the carriage and planted his legs firmly on the two sides of the aisle.

"Mother Russia welcomes you with frostly breath, comrades. Enjoy it. It is better, I assure you, than the warm breath of the German dogs on your backs, ah?" He was smiling a wide smile under a thick, Stalin-style moustache. His eyes were dark and slightly slanted at the corners. His face, wrinkled and weather-beaten, was dark too, and robustly handsome. He nodded at the tired and dirty faces around him.

"Some trip for you, poor Jewish devils. And you have not seen the end of it yet. Wait till you get to Siberia . . . Nobody's told you yet how lucky you are. Nobody's told you, so I will. And what I have to tell you is that your are coming to a land of happiness."

He looked around to examine the impression his words were making. But some people did not understand Russian, and some were too tired to pay attention. Nevertheless he went on, unmindful.

"Yes, comrades, you may not believe it, but we are happy here. This is because our needs are small, unlike you, capitalists. We are happy when we have a piece of bread to eat, when there is a tiny bit of vodka to cheer us up. And you are going to be happy with us!"

An old man who was sitting on the bench behind ours, his face swathed in bandages, murmured, "Let the devil take their happiness. Couldn't he wait with his propaganda till after breakfast? It's hard to take on an empty stomach."

A voice from the rack shushed him and a man on our left said to him in Polish, "Be quiet, old fool! The commandant is offering you happiness and you complain. It's better to be named a 'com-rade' than a 'corpse,' so smile nicely at the commandant and keep your bandaged mouth shut."

The official stood there for a while, nodding his head, then he turned and proceeded towards the other end of the carriage. I followed him with my eyes and I saw him proceeding slowly, then stopping at the end of the carriage and eyeing something in-tently. I climbed up on the bench to see what it was he was staring at and saw that it was Robert Engel. He was squeezed into the back corner of the carriage sitting on top of his valises.

The valises took the place of two people and their gleaming surfaces contrasted with the shabby surroundings and with Engel's stained jacket.

The official placed himself solidly in front of Engel. Engel did not move. He was totally absorbed in a small book he was holding to the dim light. His head was moving up and down rhythmically, as if he were trying to memorize the lines.

All the eyes turned, curious, towards them. Engel went on reading, oblivious to all, and the official just stood there patiently, cocking his head once to the left, then to the right, as if he were looking at a strange bird that just perched on a branch of a tree. His patience ended after a while, for he cried loudly, "Wake up, comrade, wake up and talk to us!"

Engel lifted his head abruptly, like a man rudely awakened from a pleasant dream. His yellow eyes blinked behind the gold frames, then filled with fear.

"Yes commandant, what is it you wish from me?"

Instead of an answer the official produced out if his breast-pocket a crumpled scrap of paper, a pouch of tobacco and a box of matches. He leaned against the frame of the door, rolled a cigarette, then lit a match by striking it against the sole of his boot. He then blew a cloud of smoke into Engel's face.

"Learned Comrade," he said mockingly. "A fine place comrade found for his studies. I modestly presume the best in the country. I am sorry the light we provide here is inadequate, the heat insufficient and the stench just a tiny bit overpowering."

Engel opened his eyes wide, uncomprehending. He did not answer, only squinted and cupped his ear. The official drew near him and looked at him fiercely.

"I see the learned comrade is carrying his burial caskets with him, ah?" He examined the shining locks on the valises, then pulled on the metal band. "How long you have been dragging those with you across Russia is one thing I wish to know. And the second is how you managed to get on the train, ah?" Thousands of men lie under bare skies all over the land, people travel on roofs of wagons, we are all crowded here like spider's eggs in a pouch and comrade is riding on top of fancy black valises like a bloody aristocrat. I hope comrade has gold and diamonds inside. Anyhow, whatever it is I wish not to see it anymore. Next stop,

37

out you go with the valises, or out go the valises and you stay with your small volume!"

I was afraid for Engel and watched the two intently. But Engel seemed to be regaining his composure. He straightened his back and put his hand on his breast-pocket.

"But . . . but . . . comrade commandant . . . it . . . it is . . . very important . . . ominously so . . ." he stumbled in broken Russian. "Here . . . the certificate . . . you may read yourself."

He fished out of his pocket a folded sheet of paper and handed it to the Russian. The official unfolded it and glanced at the bottom of the page.

"A round stamp . . . it bears a round stamp!" someone said. A round stamp was a sacred testimony to the fact that someone in the complicated hierarchy of Russian bureaucracy had dealt with the problem and issued a document.

The official seemed surprised, but he folded the paper and made a motion of resignation with his hand.

"There are some things in this life I shall never understand," he said, "and this is one of them."

Before moving on he knocked on the side of the valises. The muted sound testified that they were solidly packed.

The train moved on relentlessly, day and night, stopping once in a while at small stations in the middle of nowhere. After a few days the wide expanses of whiteness had disappeared and we entered mountainous arid terrain. Sunshine started penetrating in thin slanted beams into the wagon. It seemed to melt some of the weariness and the fear. There were deep caves in the barren mountains gaping dark and mysterious, swirling water and strangely dressed people riding small agile horses. People seemed to unfold, become willing to share. Arms stretched from one compartment to another offering cigarettes, bundles were untwisted to dig out dried fruits and candies. It was still cold, but dry. We were crossing the boundaries of Europe and entering Asia.

Groups of people took turns by the window to admire the changing and beautiful landscape. I stood glued to the window too. It was like entering a story land.

At night the train rattled on narrow tracks. The darkness around was so complete that I thought there were only the few of us, the train and the stars left in the world. People around sighed and grunted and whispered, cigarettes glowed in the darkness and the *machorka* tobacco gave a strong aroma, like that of burning dry leaves.

Mother had a candle with her. From a lump of clay she had dug from a little hill at one of the stations she had formed a candleholder with a curved handle. She put the candleholder on top of a valise, protecting the feeble, shaky flames with the palms of her hands. Cupped around the candle her hands were red and almost transparent.

A few people moved closer to us. The light of the candle made the wrinkles on their faces look deeper and their eyes darker. Looking into the flame Mother said, "We are entering a magnificent land."

The eyes turned curiously towards her. I slipped off my father's knees to be nearer. Mother then said we were in Uzbeckistan. The people opened their eyes even wider. They had never heard of this land. She then told them it was an ancient, fertile and beautiful country, of mild climate and protected from harsh winds and enemies by high mountains. It was a part of Russia now, but hundreds of years ago, it was the proudest of lands, a centre of the Empire of the Mamluks, who came from the east and conquered those territories like a hurricane. She told them about the wild Gingis Han and the wise Tamerlane who ruled amidst unbelievable splendours.

The man with the bandaged face, who used to be a butcher's helper in the small Jewish town from which he escaped scratched his ear thoughtfully.

"And where do you know all this from, Mrs. Solomonovna? How does one know things like this?"

"I read about it, Mr. Kugelman."

"And you believe what you read?"

"Just as much as I believe what I hear, and sometimes more."

Mr. Kugelman smiled. "I can see that when asked, you can answer, Mrs. Solomonovna. But if you ask *me*, *I* don't believe in any reading. What is reading good for? It is like the wind passing over a field of wheat. You can't eat it, you can't drink it, you can't sleep with it or use it for a blanket at night. But take, for example, a nice side of rib . . . "

Mother sighed, though I could see that the thought of a nice side of rib was not unpleasant to her. "It would take too long to explain, Mr. Kugelman. You are certainly right about some things. And yet, Mr. Kugelman, if it weren't for the wind, could the clouds accumulate and cause rain to fall?"

Mr. Kugelman scratched his ear again. "You are a difficult person to argue with, Mrs. Solomonovna."

"This is because I read a lot, Mr. Kugelman."

"But anyway, you do not convince me."

Other voices came from the darkened part of the carriage.

"Reading is empty words on paper to confuse your mind when your stomach is empty."

"No child was ever born from reading."

"Our Rabbi read all his life. So the Germans dragged him away from the reading stand. We did not read. We hid in the forest."

I looked at Mother. She seemed lost. I was sorry for her. It seemed strange to me; here she was telling them beautiful stories and they all turned against her. But I could also see that what they said was true. You really could not eat stories. The Rabbi did not run to the forest. As for the children, my mother did have one though she read.

Then a voice came from the other end of the carriage.

"And yet," the voice said, "all of you listened intently, with your eyes and ears wide open. It was so quiet around. It looked as if you forgot everything else."

It was such a loud and clear voice, that at first I did not identify it as belonging to Robert Engel. I was grateful to him. Mother seemed grateful too, for she smiled and the thin wrinkles disappeared from her forehead. The others did not react. Then she blew the candle out.

Other than that one strong reaction, Engel seemed oblivious to all. Whenever I looked in his direction, more to see the valises than to see him, he was perched on top of them, like a strange bird, almost immobile in his hawklike position, his head bent above his small volume. People were making bets about the contents of his suitcases. Mr. Kugelman said it was tobacco. The skinny man who slept on top of the luggage rack said it was furs. Others were divided between meat, conserves and beans. But

40

soon they lost interest in him. Only the Russian official still bothered to tease him and cause a thin smile to linger on Engel's lips for a while.

Engel was not very talkative, but after a while we did learn a few things about him. He told Mother that he came from a Polish town close to the German border. He told Father that he had been a lonely bachelor all his life. It looked as if everything he had was locked in those fancy valises. He often examined them with fondness, and, one could say, a certain degree of respect. He spread a blanket on them at night and then slept curled up on top. He had no food with him and was living on whatever the authorities rationed, which was not much. As they said in Russia—too much to die on and not enough to live on. A kind hand sometimes offered him tea leaves or a few dried tomatoes, and he accepted hastily and with some embarrassment. At the stations where we disembarked to trade cigarettes and tobacco for food, he stayed inside, guarding his black treasures.

"Learned Comrade," the official teased him, "take care not to stay too long on top of these valises. Your behind may stick to the lid and then you may have some trouble opening them. And then what. . . ?"

Engel usually shied away from the adults in the company. Only two other children and I were allowed to share his seat on top of the valises, close to the ceiling. He was fond of children. Sometimes, when he tired of looking into his small book, when his eyes were red and swollen under the gold-rimmed glasses, he told us stories. It was he who first told me the story of Aladdin and his lamp. When he described the lamp, which was made of brass, his eyes wandered to the shiny locks on his valises.

Then, one day he said something strange, something I wished I could believe. He said there were many lamps like Aladdin's around, but people did not know where to look for them. "I hope," he said to us, "I hope you find yours one day."

Once, when I thought he was in a better mood than usual, I pulled on his sleeve to divert his attention from his small volume and then, slowly and hesitantly, I asked him what it was that was hidden in his valises. I did not believe for a moment, I said, that those where furs or conserves, the way others did. So what

41

was it? I asked. Were those princess's garments entrusted to his care or perhaps some secrets of a powerful king? Was he, Engel, an important person in disguise?

He smiled slyly and his eyes narrowed under his gold-rimmed glasses. "So you want to know everything, eh? So curiosity is eating at your heart like a green worm?"

I lowered my eyes innocently and started fingering the button of his jacket. "I just want to know, Uncle Engel. Just in case you do not mind telling me. I'll keep it a secret, I promise."

He observed me for a while, as if trying to decide what to do next, then threw a quick glance around and bent his head towards me. "Could you not guess till now?" he whispered, "It's the complete pre-war production of Aladdin's lamps. I am salvaging them from Hitler."

I looked at him with disbelief, but he only smiled slyly again, then went on reading in his little book, which had minute letters, very thin pages and a nice leather cover.

One day we arrived at a train station in a city, the name of which was Samarkand. The station was large and had a few lines of tracks and some solid whitewashed buildings. We were told to disembark for de-lousing, showers and rest. We crawled out of the wagons, stretching our limbs, basking in the luxury of fresh air. Our scanty belongings were to go with us to the disinfection centre. Rumours spread that typhoid and cholera were rampant in the area. Lice were the chief transmitters of these diseases and we all knew that we were infested. Engel was the last to emerge, his thin frame almost bent under the weight of the valises.

People were now emerging from the other wagons and the platform was soon noisy and crowded. Somebody coughed into the loudspeakers. The sound reverberated across the platform, silencing everybody. Then a voice announced a list of people who were to report to the station's commanding officer immediately. Robert Engel was one of the first. He was standing not far from us, and I noticed his desperate, confused expression. Others were already on their way, running towards the large building in the centre of the complex. He seemed to be weighing something in his mind. He tried to lift the valises, then approached a man on his left. The man shrugged his shoulders, as if reluctant to take it upon himself, then agreed to keep an eye on them.

Engel joined the others, turning to look back every few steps. He seemed desperately torn between the need to obey and the will to return. But like all of us he knew that one did not disobey the authorities for any reason in the world and, casting one last glance backwards, he entered the building.

Shortly afterwards, the loudspeakers directed us to the exit, where trucks were standing ready to transport us to the disinfection centre. The man assigned to watch the valises tried to lift them, but they were too heavy and he proceeded without them. The line of people divided, leaving them behind.

We saw Engel later that afternoon in the disinfection centre. With swollen eyes, his hands moving wildly, he was running from person to person.

"Have you seen my valises?" he cried. "Have you seen my valises!" Nobody had seen them after leaving the station. He returned to the platform, then came back, dishevelled, tearful, desperate. He held his head between his hands.

"They stole my valises!" he cried. "They stole my valises!"

He ran back and forth, asking questions, still hopeful, then collapsed on the floor. He sat there crouched and broken. People were passing by, nodding, moving on. Mr. Kugelman approached him and laid a hand on his shoulder.

"Calm down, Mr. Engel, calm down. Myself and other people lost families and homes and they are not that desperate. What was it that you kept in those valises?"

Robert Engel lifted his face and, slowly, as if every syllable was causing him pain, uttered, "My books, all my books." The old man retreated smiling cynically.

Someone started laughing loudly, then someone else joined in. Word passed around and after a while there was a crowd of people standing laughing, unfeeling. Engel stared at them blankly, unseeing, unhearing, engulfed by despair.

"My books," he repeated, "my research, my life's work, all gone."

Nobody seemed to understand. I too stared at him in astonishment and fear. But the intensity of his anguish touched me in a strange way. I wanted to run to him, to put my arms around him, to tell him not to cry, that perhaps he would find his valises. But I was too shy and I remained in the distance, just staring at him, like the others.

The train continued on its way, but we decided to remain in that city. It was a beautiful city and it was the ancient capital of the conqueror Tamerlane.

Engel stayed too, hoping to locate his valises. He posted notices everywhere, promised rewards and gratitude.

He found work as a water carrier and I met him often on my way to school. He had to balance two metal buckets suspended from a long wooden pole that rested on his shoulders. He carried the water from the public cistern, next to the train station, and people jokingly said that he hoped to empty the cistern to find out if the valises were at its bottom.

"Not much of a difference," he remarked to me once. "I used to quench people's thirst for knowledge, now I quench their thirst for water. One can't live without either."

I was one of the few who would still listen to his oft-repeated story. The grownups had their own problems and Engel's loss seemed to them to be trivial and unimportant. I too could not understand the depth of his despair. People were dying in the streets, husbands and fathers were going to war—maybe never to return—and he was still mourning his books. People said he was an "old *nudnick*" —a bore—and though I liked Engel, deep within myself I was starting to agree with them.

But one day I saw things differently. At the school for refugee children, the ones who did best in their studies were given a special privilege: they could borrow a Polish book from the principal's office and take it home for a few days. There were only five or six books in the principal's glass case and he handed them out with reverence and many words of admonition. I received *The Fairy Tales* of Oscar Wilde—a beautiful old book, illustrated with dreamy prictures in tones of gold, light blue and purple. I read while walking and eating, and also stealthily at night, under the blanket or the dim light of the kerosene lamp. I cried with the Happy Prince and the swallow, laughed at the unfriendly miller; the mermaid and the selfish giant followed me wherever I went. For a few days I lived in an enchanted world.

44

One evening I went down to the square, where I played with the neighbourhood children, to show the book to my friend Samenchuk. I lay the book on the step, next to where we were sitting and I forgot it there. I remembered it only after I returned home. I immediately ran back to the square. But the book was not there. I spent a tormented, sleepless night. In my nightmares I saw my parents stooping above me with angry and disappointed faces. I saw the principal's finger, long and accusing, pointing in the direction of the empty space in the glass case. I thought with sorrow that I should never again be given the privilege of taking home any of the other books he held there. I knew the children were going to nickname me "the book loser" and that the nickname would stay with me forever.

But even more painful was the realization that I would never know what happened to the mermaid, or to the characters in the other, unread stories. I had a feeling of being left suspended in a void and I cried over their fates and mine.

The next day, my eyes still red and swollen, I ran after the water carrier. "Uncle Engel, stop, stop!" I wanted to tell him about the book, to ask whether he knew the end, whether he had read the other stories. I was gasping and puffing when I reached him. He paused and looked at me surprised.

"What is it, my child?" His gold frames sparkled in the sun.

"Uncle Engel, I . . . lost a book. Oscar Wilde. Do you know the stories?"

I wanted to tell him more, but something held me back. Perhaps it was the memory of the scene in the disinfection centre.

He stooped above me. "You did? Oscar Wilde, you say? No. I do not know his stories. Never read them. But don't be sad." He patted my head softly. "You know, when the war ends and you come back to Poland, the stores are going to be loaded with books. All you'll have to do is walk up to the lady at the counter, and she will bring them to you. There are going to be libraries too, with miles and miles of books, on many bright floors. In the corner, just next to the window, you'll find Oscar Wilde's stories . . . with beautiful colourful pictures . . . you'll see."

It sounded impossible, but nice. Then he said quietly, sadly, "As for me, it's all lost."

45

"No, it's not, Uncle Engel, it's not!" I cried. "Remember Aladdin's lamp!"

Then I ran away, embarrassed by my audacity. When I looked back he was still standing there, shading his eyes with his hands, the dark surface of water in the buckets sparkling and shimmering.

THE HAIRCUT

Immediately after Claudia Ivanovna, the head teacher of the Communist Worker's Kindergarten of Samarkand, entered my name into the thick school book with the dark cover, Mother and I headed towards Brothers Skiller's Barbershop. When we arrived, after the long trek through the narrow alleys of the Old City, I was still hurting from the rough treatment Claudia Ivanovna had given my hair, and her heavy throaty voice still rang in my ears.

"A haircut!" she said. "A haircut will be absolutely necessary as a condition for admission."

The heavy wooden door of Brothers Skiller's Barbershop was locked from the inside. Mother knocked. I heard the metallic sound of a latch being opened and we were let in. The air in the shop was humid, mildewy and smelled of sweaty bodies sprinkled with cologne. I knew this smell well. I knew it from the train which had brought us here not so long ago. The fat woman who shared our platform in the cattle wagon in which we travelled had a large bottle in her bag.

The bottle was light green and had a picture of lilies of the valley on the label. The woman sweated a lot, even when it was cold in the wagon. From time to time she took the bottle out of her bag and very carefully poured some drops into the crevice between her breasts. Warm wafts of sweetish air reached us as she fanned herself with a newspaper and my father would turn his head in discomfort.

"You smell like a flower in an outhouse, Mrs. Milstein." a burly man on the upper deck said to her once, and everybody laughed, but Mrs. Milstein blushed and was sad.

But here it smelled different. It was a sharp and cold smell. It seemed to be coming out of the whitewashed walls, out of the tattered towels that hung from a rusty nail and from the stained covers of the armchairs. It seemed to be coming from the white uniforms of the two brothers, one of whom addressed Mother in Russian. "A haircut for the little one, Madame Solomonovna? But of course. Nothing could give us more pleasure."

I looked up. The two of them were standing above me like two exclamation marks. Their big smiles revealed four rows of huge yellow teeth with dark gaps in between. They were almost exactly alike: of the same height, both had round eyes that looked like pale green marbles about to pop out and roll to the ground. Their hair was black, smooth and shiny, divided in the middle and held down by a dark net tied in a bow at the back.

I did not like the two brothers Skiller, though it was the first time I was seeing them face to face. I had seen them before, standing behind their shop window. I used to pass by the shop frequently on my way to the large yard at the end of the boulevard. There were children to play with in that yard. In our yard there were only adults. Whenever I passed by, they were there, stationed in the window like two black and white mannequins. It was a strange shop they had. There were no shelves there, no sacks of flour or potatoes, and no customers. All I could see were the armchairs, the mirrors and three leather belts on the wall. At first I waved at the brothers Skillers, but they never waved back. So I stopped waving, but they went on ogling me with their big round eyes.

But that was not the main reason for my dislike. I started disliking them when they told on me to Mother. I knew that telling on someone was the worst thing one person could do to another person. We had a name for people like this out in the yard and it was not a nice name. I remembered what I saw in the small Russian town where we stopped on our way here. They were taking a man out of a police station. He was handcuffed and blindfolded and was followed by two soldiers with guns. He was screaming, "I did not tell! I did not tell!" A girl who was standing next to me said: "He is going to be killed. He is a bad man. He told something he should not have told!"

There was a large puddle right in front of the brothers' shop. It was not one of those deep puddles where the leg sinks to mid calf, nor one of the very shallow ones where there is hardly any water. I liked to cross that puddle very slowly, to see my shoes go deeper and deeper in the water till only the tops were visible. The water bubbled, ripples formed on the surface. The stirred mud came up like smoke out of the bottle of the Thief of Bagdad, then formed yellow leaves and flowers that dissolved and sank when I stood still. The water felt tepid and tickled my feet. When I got out to the sidewalk my shoes felt soggy and were full of muddy water that came out through the lace holes in small funny squirts. I knew Mother was not going to be happy to see the shoes wet, so I put them under the bed as soon as I came home. I managed to hide them from her for a while.

But one day she came in and I could see the brewing storm on her face. Her lips were closed so tightly they looked as if she never intended to open them again. She then stooped and crouched next to my bed. In a rapid motion she brought the shoes out. They were greenish with mildew, creased like the face of an old lady whose tongue is sticking out, their soles a gaping mouth, the laces limp and tattered. The next thing I knew, the shoes were flying to the corner of the room and Mother's hand was reaching for my collar, lifting me off my seat and placing me on her knees, my behind exposed and jutting out. She started beating it mercilessly, all the while yelling as if it was she who was being hit and not me. She yelled something about the jacket she had sold to buy me the shoes, and about God having sent her a punishment for uncommitted sins in the shape of me, and about how she should have thought twice before she brought me into the world and instead had not thought even once.

"Promise you will never do it again!" she yelled.

It hurt and I yelled, "I won't! I won't ever! I promise I won't!" But she did not believe me and she hit me again and again.

"Thank goodness for the brothers Skiller!" she shouted. "If it were not for them, I would have remained ignorant till the summer and you would have had no shoes, as if that mess could be still called shoes!"

They were the ones who told her, they were the ones.

I undressed, hurting and shivering, and crawled into my bed promising revenge. From then on, whenever I headed for the yard I crossed to the other side of the boulevard. Once I passed by the shop with Mother and I stuck my tongue at them. But they only went on staring sheepishly at me. At that time I did not yet know that theirs was a barbershop. So I asked Mother.

"If they have nothing to sell," I said, "why do they have a shop? And why are there no customers in the store?"

Mother laughed and said it was a barbershop, a place where people came to have their hair cut. As for customers, most came after work, in the evening, or before work, very early in the morning.

It seemed strange to me one needed a shop with a large window to do haircuts. The only haircutting I had seen done was out in the fresh air, when we were waiting for a train at the station in Kiev. A line of soldiers formed in front of a uniformed small man with a moustache and a huge mane of black hair. He was sitting next to a small table on top of which were large scissors, a bowl of soapy water and a small instrument with claws. The soldiers sat on a metal chair that was placed right there on the platform and the man shaved their heads clean. "Like a knee," my mother said. After a while there was a heap of hair around the chair, brown, blond and black. A gust of wind came and the hair started whirling around, getting into our eyes and noses. Mother covered my face with a hankerchief. The soldiers looked strange without their hair. They looked much more yellow than before and their teeth showed large when they smiled. When they came back to their group they were greeted with laughs. The soldiers tapped each other's heads as if they were drums.

But the kerchiefed women who sat leaning against the gray stone columns of the station, surrounded by bundles and small children, did not laugh at all. They said some strange things and the words they uttered had the bitter taste of the soup they gave us at the refugees' center. They said the barber was fitting the soldiers for their dance with death. I did not understand what they meant, but their words had a shrill cutting sound.

"They are lining up for it, *batyushka*," they said. "They are in a hurry. And who would be surprised? In this kind of world, is there a chance? Is there a chance for us at all?" The women looked at the soldiers sadly and wiped the green snot from the children's faces with the sleeves of their jackets.

But the soldiers were not sad. They pranced about and laughed as if they did not share the women's concern. The boat-shaped hats were too large for their bald heads. They tried to twist the hats into shape, but gave it up after a while and just let them fall over their foreheads. Before they boarded the train an orchestra came and played a soft melody and they threw their hats up in the air. Some hats fell in the laps of the squatting women. The women got up to their feet and put the hats on those big bald heads. The soldiers, who were taller, stooped and kissed the women and then disappeared in the clouds of smoke that came from under the train.

I myself had never had a haircut, at least not one that I could remember. My hair was blond and curly and fell to my shoulders. It seemed to attract more attention than the rest of me. Mother was telling everybody how my old nanny used to take care of it and wash it with camomile. Women in Russia used to approach us in the street and touch my hair with the tips of their red wrinkled fingers. "Silk," they said. "Real silk." On the army truck going to Kiev a soldier asked Father to let him hold me with the hand that was not holding the gun. He caressed my hair and balanced me on his knee tenderly.

"My little girl has hair like this too, though not so curly," he said. And then, looking out into the darkness he said, "Who knows whether I shall ever see her again?" He wore a helmet and I knew he did not have any hair underneath. I also knew that I should never allow anyone to cut my hair. I saw a young woman once who had thick braids that reached the small of her back. She smiled happily. I knew that those long braids had something to do with that smile, though she was also holding a large loaf of bread which she managed to get after a long wait in line. The lovely young women in Samarkand had dozens of thin braids falling to their shoulders. I wanted to have braids like theirs one day.

But my hopes were cut short by Claudia Ivanovna and by the fact that I had to start going to kindergarten. Mother started working full time after Father went into the army. She left home in the morning and returned after dusk. When she left she locked the door behind her. Our room was small, very dark and almost empty. I stayed there alone till she came back from work, late in the afternoon. Sometimes I ran after her, clinging to her skirt.

"Don't leave, Mother, I am afraid to stay alone."

But she would force my hand open. "I'll be an hour only . . . "

"A short hour, or a long hour, Mother?"

"As short as I can make it."

It was usually a very long hour that stretched without end. I walked back and forth in the small room like a cat in a cage, then squatted in the corner. Sometimes I closed my eyes and thought about how it was going to be when we returned to Poland, to my old nanny and to the small house with a garden, where we lived. I was certain it would come, but it all seemed far far away.

One day Mother came home in a better mood than usual. She announced there was a kindergarten that had just opened and that we would be going to register the next morning. She said it was hard to get a referral for someone who was not a member of the party, but that Dr. Golubeyev, director of the school where she worked, had graciously agreed to give her a letter.

She boiled a big pot of water on the kerosene burner and took out of the valise a small bar of white soap, the last one we had from Poland. It was wrapped in a scarf and kept for special occasions only. She then placed a metal basin in the middle of the room. She scrubbed me first with the rough brown soap that had some sand in it till I was red, then finished me off with the sweet smelling one. She washed my hair in the same water. After she washed her hair too, she put on her dress. Then she sat at the table and stared at the door as if she expected some important visitor to come in.

On the next morning she scrubbed my face again, put on her Sunday dress with white and purple tulips, tied her hair in a bun, checked my ears and warned me to behave.

I was happy too. It was not often that I went anywhere with Mother. My outings were confined to visits to the neighboring yard. I was looking forward to a walk through the farther streets of town, which were humming with colourful people and where one could see varied goods displayed in the stalls: raisins in brown sacks and dried strips of melon and nuts, figs and dates and dark red pomegranates, which sparkled like rubies. The boulevard where we lived was in the modern section of town. It seemed quiet, sad and empty compared to the streets of the beautiful old town where the Uzbecks lived.

We first walked along the wide Gorky Avenue. The acacia trees stood bare and gray, their branches hanging limply like thin long fingers. Drops of morning rain fell like large tears. The earth was almost dry, the rain water having gathered in fast little streams on the side of the road. A woman came from the opposite direction, patted my head and smiled at us.

"Sweet girl you have, citizen."

"Sometimes sweet and sometimes not so sweet," Mother answered.

The woman gave her a curious glance and continued on her way. We turned into a narrow street at the corner of which an old Uzbeck woman sold yellowish root-mousse in cones made of thin bark. My mouth watered, but I knew Mother wouldn't buy me any. The street was so narrow that we had to stand glued against a wall whenever a cart or a camel came from the other direction. We rubbed shoulders with veiled women in long capes and with pretty girls in colourful dresses. Then the street opened into a small market square where turbaned old men displayed brass pitchers and long-necked samovars, gracefully curved and richly carved with flowers and letters. Younger men turned pieces of meat on large skewers that rested on containers with coals. But those were things that only the rich could afford. I knew the Thief from Bagdad would have felt at home here and so would Aladdin with his lamp.

Mother asked for directions and we turned into another street, at the end of which stood a large whitewashed building. There was a sentry in a small booth at the gate. He wore a hat with wide flaps and his hands were buried inside his sleeves to keep warm. He glanced at the paper Mother handed him and let us in. Shortly afterwards we stood in front of a dark door at the end of a long corridor.

"Claudia Ivanovna, Head Teacher, it's here," Mother said. She knocked on the door and we were let in by a tall woman with square shoulders and breasts that hung like udders under a gray sweater. She had a long nose, smooth black hair cut short just beneath her ears and she wore heavy men's shoes over thick woollen stockings. She shook mother's hand energetically and motioned to me to come in and sit on a chair across from hers. She motioned to Mother to remain seated close to the entrance where a small bench was placed beneath a hanger with black umbrellas that looked like long birds hanging with their heads down. Beside the umbrellas and Claudia Ivanovna's table the room was quite empty. The walls were bare except for a large portrait of Stalin, almost life-size. He smiled benignly under his heavy moustache and held his hand inside his jacket. His chest was decorated with many medals and multi-colored ribbons, and his pants were well ironed—unlike those of most of the men I had seen.

Claudia Ivanovna kept looking for something in her drawer. She then brought out a pen, an inkpot made of aluminum and a large notebook that opened to a page covered with letters. She looked the page up and down, then glanced at me abruptly. "So," she paused to look at me again. "So this is our new student." She leaned backwards in her chair, as if she wanted to have a better look at me from a distance. I blinked and pushed my chest forward a little, the way I had seen young pioneers of the Communist party do on posters.

Mother got up from her bench and approached the table in small steps, her lips in a thin smile. "Yes, Claudia Ivanovna, please, it's very important that she gets accepted. A child her age, you know . . . education is important, and of course the beautiful Russian language. When we leave, I want her to take this treasure from here . . . Pushkin, Gogol, Lermontov . . . " She raised her eyes to the ceiling, as if summoning the help of the celebrated writers. "How important for a young mind . . . "

Claudia Ivanovna was of a more practical turn of mind. "Did you bring the letters of recommendation and the documents?" she asked.

"But of course . . . " Mother opened her bag and shakily extracted a bundle of papers.

Claudia Ivanovna looked through the papers carefully, passing her finger over her tongue whenever she turned a page. She examined the round stamps on the documents, put some papers up to the light, then compared my face to the photograph in a small booklet.

"Everything in order," she said to Mother and handed her the papers.

Now she is going to question me, I thought fearfully. And that will be the end of me.

But instead Claudia Ivanovna motioned to me to approach her. She moved her chair away from the table, spread her legs and drew me between her thick thighs. Her sharp eyes scanned my face, then scrutinized my head. Without a word she pushed me back, brought her knees together, and forced my head into her lap. My nose was pressed between her thighs. It was dark in Claudia Ivanovna's lap and it smelled bad. I wanted to get out, I wanted to know what she was going to do to me, but my head was pressed firmly down. I tried to hold onto the rungs of her chair, but she pulled my hands away.

"Stay there!" she said in a stern voice. "And keep your head where it belongs or else!"

She brought her head closer to mine and I could smell her breath. There was a bit of garlic in it and some vodka and on the whole it was unpleasant.

"A stubborn one you've brought up, Madame Solomonovna!" I heard her addressing Mother. "Small, blue-eyed like an angel, but stubborn like a baby goat. What we'll do here, in our school, is snip the little horns and you'll bless us for it."

A murmur of assent came from Mother's corner. I was frightened. What was it she was saying? That I was growing horns like a goat? I reached to touch my head, but Claudia Ivanovna's hand was there before mine. Next thing her fingers were running on top of my scalp like ants. She was parting my hair with her fingers. Then she took something out of her drawer. It was a metal comb. I felt sharp teeth going through my hair and scratching the skin, while Claudia Ivanovna's fingers executed a wild dance around them.

Then she exclaimed victoriously "Just what I thought!" and the wild dance stopped.

She must have found the horn. I hear mother's feet clap-clapping on the floor. I heard something snapping between Claudia Ivanovna's fingernails. "A big and juicy one!" she said with apparent relish.

My heart sank within me. Mother was hovering nearby, I could hear her rapid, tense breath. My nose struggled in the crevice between Claudia Ivanovna's thighs. She kept searching for something on my head, but failing to find anything new she spread her legs and let me out into the fresh air. She raked my hair with her fingers and turned me towards Mother.

Mother was standing in front of the table guiltily and dejectedly, her small old handbag dangling limply from her arm.

"*Da, da,* Claudia Ivanovna," she stuttered."*Vy pravy.*" she said. "You're right." "But it's ... it's ... only one, a solitary specimen."

"One is enough to bring typhoid on the whole school!" the headteacher said sternly.

Mother hung her head down and I stood between the two of them, not knowing what to do with myself.

"Yes, Claudia Ivanovna." Mother said.

"The only solution will be a haircut!" The head teacher's fingers crisscrossed menacingly on the top of my head.

"Till tomorrow then, Claudia Ivanovna."

"Yes, till tomorrow." She followed us to the door.

We went down the stairs. On the landing there was another portrait of Stalin hanging above a metal spittoon. This time he was holding in his arms a little pigtailed girl with a bouquet of flowers and his face was oozing fatherly delight.

"Stalin here, Stalin there, Stalin watching everywhere."

Mother hummed quietly and smirked. But at that moment Stalin was of no great concern to me. My mind was occupied with anxious thoughts that had little to do with the head of state. I stopped under the portrait and looked up at Mother.

"Was it big, Mother, tell me the truth?"

"Yes, fairly big."

"And dark too?"

"So-so, kind of grayish."

"Is it going to grow any bigger?"

"Is what going to grow any bigger?"

"The horn, mother, the horn she found on my head."

Mother looked at me with amazement. "I don't know what you are talking about. It was lice she found."

"Oh, lice, like the people on the train had? The ones that were scratching themselves all the time?"

"Yes, the same."

I was relieved and saddened at the same time. Lice were better than horns, but lice were not such good news either.

"So what are we going to do about them? Can we chase them away? Will you wash my hair in kerosene, the way Mrs. Milstein did?"

"No. That's not what Claudia Ivanovna demands. Didn't you hear? She wants you to have your hair cut. We are going to see the brothers Skiller right away."

"Will it hurt, Mother?"

"No, silly."

"Will they take all my hair away?"

"No, they'll . . . " she hesitated for a minute. "They'll just shorten your hair a little and that will be it." She turned her face away and we headed towards the gate.

The walls of Brothers Skiller's shop were whitewashed over an uneven rough surface that looked like a pockmarked face. The three black leather belts were still there; from the inside they looked larger and darker. On a glass shelf suspended by heavy strings there were small bottles filled with coloured liquids, dark green, yellow and milky white. The mirrors on the wall were old, their corners black and their surfaces spotted with many black dots. The armchairs were upholstered in black leather, veined like a palm of a dark hand, and had shiny metal knobs and levers. I could see my face in one of the knobs. It looked like a round curly ball with an enormous nose.

One of the brothers reached for my hand. I stepped back and hid my hand behind my back. He grimaced helplessly, his eyes summoning Mother's intervention. The lump on his throat wobbled and his eyes seemed even rounder.

"Climb on top of this chair!" Mother hissed. "The good

brothers do not have a whole day to waste on you."

I stepped on top of a small stool which one of the brothers pushed towards me with his foot. A wooden board rested on the arms of the chair. I sat on it stiffly and looked into the large spotted mirror. I was perched high and alone. In the foreground were the brothers Skiller and my mother. They had strange strained smiles on their faces. The three belts were on the wall behind them. A paper fly-trap was suspended from a bare electric bulb, just behind my head, dead flies stretching their skinny legs from its yellowish sticky surface.

The skinnier of the two brothers took a pair of shiny scissors out of a small cabinet. He spat on the blade, then sharpened it on one of the belts. He came nearer. His face was close to mine and I could see the veins beneath his pale skin, and the ends of dark hair on his face. He stooped and turned the knob on the side of the chair. I observed him turning the knob for a while. When he stopped and I raised my head, I saw I was not facing the mirror. Instead I was facing Mother and the stouter brother, who were sitting on a bench placed against the wall.

"Why did you turn me away?" I yelled. "Why can't I look in the mirror?"

Brother Skiller paused, looked at Mother, then in a kind tone said, "Don't be afraid, little girl. It is easier for me to do your haircut this way. It's mainly because of this board that we must use because you are so little. In olden times we used to have a handsome horse for children. But it had a high content of brass and they took it away, you see, to use, for the army . . . "

I could not understand why they needed a barber's horse in the army, but then they took my father too and I could not understand why. But this explanation calmed me down a little.

The brother took out a big white piece of material and tucked it under my chin. It felt cold and refreshing. He started whistling then. The melody was nice and sounded familiar. I smiled.

The second brother Skiller was fast to notice.

"That's a nice girl. She smiled finally. So now we are going to be a nice little girl till we're finished. Right?" The three of them were showing their teeth in big, sweet smiles. The smiles of the two brothers had a yellowish tint, and my mother's was gray-purplish, like the tulips on her dress. I wanted to answer, but I did not, for at that very moment I saw a blond curl roll down the white bib and onto the earthen floor. Then came the next and then another and another. They were falling fast now. The hand of brother Skiller, cold and bony, was pressing on my skull, bending it down till my face was almost buried in the white cloth. It was strangely quiet around me. I felt hair in my eyes and in my mouth. Small wisps seemed to be floating in the air, then to fall down like golden rain. The blades of the scissors touched my skull. I felt cold all of a sudden. It was cold around my head. The metal blades seemed to be touching it more and more often. I wanted to touch it too, but I was swathed in white cloth and my head was held tightly by the big fingers of brother Skiller.

"Two more minutes, little girl, and we are finished, just two more minutes."

He was whistling some fast melody now, very fast and the blades moved to the rhythm of his whistling—click, click, click— and I was colder and colder and more and more tired.

Finally brother Skiller stopped and stepped back, as if to admire what he had done. I could lift my face now. I looked at Mother. There was a strange expression on her face. She looked as if she too was frightened of something. When she saw me staring at her she glanced away.

The stouter brother Skiller took a rounded knife out of a leather pouch and started moving it up and down one of the belts in a slow, measured motion. I got frightened. *What was that for? What did they need a knife for?*

The skinnier brother took the knife into his hand. He noticed my frightened eyes. "It's nothing, little girl, just a few stray hairs ... it's nothing ... " The blade was shining in his hand.

A minute later I felt it going over my scalp, slowly, smoothly. *What was it?! It was as if there was nothing there!* I was alarmed. *But they said it was going to be just a little haircut.*

There was a thin mist of cologne around me.

"Finished, finished, little girl, it's all finished!" brother Skiller cried victoriously. In his hand was a heavy bottle with a green pump at the end of which dangled a silky tassel. He sprayed the air around me lavishly. Tiny drops fell on my face. I closed my eyes and felt my eyelids getting cool and moist. I saw brother

59

Skiller then untucking the white cloth and gathering it by the corners. My curls were in it and he was taking them to the garbage can. He returned, stooped again and started turning the knob. Soon I was going to see myself all new and shiny. Perhaps it would look nice. I followed his movements curiously. Then I closed my eyes. When he stopped the knob I heard him saying, "That's it, you can look now!"

I first peeped through my eyelashes. I did not see anyone I could recognize in the mirror. Then I opened my eyes wide. The thing in the mirror opened its eyes too. I opened my mouth; it opened its mouth too. I closed it back very fast. I raised my hand. It went on mimicking me. The thing in the mirror had a big round head, dark on top, nose, teeth and ears sticking out like two handles. It was pale and terrible. I moved backwards in the chair, then rubbed the hair out of my eyes. I could see clearly now ... It's impossible ... It's not ... I slid off the chair. I approached the mirror. The truth started dawning me. *Perhaps it was all a nightmare. Perhaps I could rub it off that mirror.* I scratched the glass with my fingernails. It remained cool and smooth. The big round head was staring at me with wide open huge eyes, two eyes moving wildly in front of it. I stepped away from the mirror. The head was staring at me—ugly, bald, with black patches, one of which was oozing blood.

I crouched on the floor, trying to scoop up the few remaining curls. I put them back on my head and patted them flat, hoping they would stay there. But they slipped right back to the floor.

"Give me back my hair!" I cried. "Give me back my hair, liars!" I attacked the black pants of one of the brothers with my fists.

"You said ... You said ..." I sobbed. "You said it was going to be only a small haircut!"

They stood there as if paralyzed by my outburst, their expressions cold and disapproving. I felt Mother's hand on my shoulder.

"It'll grow back, you'll see, it will grow back soon." I snatched my shoulder from her grasp and stood facing them.

"I am going to a dance with death!" I screamed. "I am going to a dance with death like the soldiers!"

They seemed taken aback, frightened.

"But child ... "

I backed away from them and in a fast motion opened the door. I ran out into the gray street with its dripping acacias and yellow tepid puddles. I wanted to run away somewhere, to the train station, to Father, who was far away, to my nanny who would wash my hair with soft camomile. I heard them running after me, screaming something in Polish and in Russian, telling me to stop, to come back, that everything was going to be alright, that my hair would grow back even more beautiful. But I kept running till I reached the locked gate of our yard.

THE STEPMOTHER

A week after Savo Djon's funeral, my mother announced that we must pay a visit of condolence to the girl's stepmother, Fatima. But I did not want to go. I ground my heels into the carpet, refused to talk to her and avoided looking into her eyes. The memory was still fresh in my mind, nightmarish and painful: the small coffin being carried away from the square, and Fatima standing there, in the midst of women dressed in blue mourning capes, as if none of it was her fault, crying and wailing as if she really cared.

Then, I had not even been allowed to go down and join the mourners. "We are not Uzbecks," Mother said. "We were not invited." Now she wanted me to go down and face Fatima, stand there not knowing what I should say or do, and listen to my mother saying things she did not mean.

"I'm not going!" I announced.

But my mother was adamant. "It's the custom," she said. "We must go and console the bereaved. Fatima is our landlady. She was kind to us. We owe her that much."

I stepped out with her into the open veranda that connected our house to that of Fatima. I had more than one reason to be unhappy with Mother. That morning I heard her talking with our neighbour, Masha Kronenberg, like us, a refugee from Poland. They agreed that after what had happened we could not possibly go on living there. I had lost my friend; now I was going to lose my beautiful bright room with the arched window looking towards the city and the little sunlit square.

I looked down. The sun was setting and the square was carpeted with long shadows. Hundreds of birds chirped loudly, settling down for the night in the mulberry trees. The street beneath was, as always, teeming with people: herdsmen driving their cattle, old turbanned men on donkeys, women in capes and veils gossiping noisily and street vendors shouting out praises of their goods. My friend Samenchuk was there, playing on the steps of the wooden mosque. In the distance the beautiful dome of Tamerlane's tomb sparkled and shone, its turquoise tiles reflecting a myriad little suns. Mother took my hand. "Let's go now!"

A minute later we were standing in front of the carved wooden door that opened into Fatima's inner yard. Mother pulled on a wire loop and a bell clanged. I still hoped that I could run away or convince Mother to go in without me. Scenes from that terrible night held on to me. It seemed that they were going to stay with me forever: Savo Djon's screams, and me lying shivering next to Mother in the dark, dogs barking, then the tumult downstairs, police questioning Fatima, her pale face illuminated by the flickering light from an old lantern, then her voice saying, "She is dead, Commandant, dead." I wished it were a dream. But it was not. I tried to wriggle my arm out of Mother's grasp, but she held me tightly by my wrist, as if she knew where my thoughts were going. She raised her other hand to ring again, but at that moment the door opened and a woman in a blue mourning cape let us in.

The inner yard of Fatima's house was suffused with the warm glow of the setting sun and smelled of herbs and roses. She sat in the middle of a raised wooden platform on a low stool. Her shoulders were hunched and her face hidden in a mass of falling gray hair. We stopped in the entrance and stood there for a while quietly. When Fatima raised her head, I gasped. She looked so many years older than she had a week ago. Her face was pale and wrinkled and her eyes were swollen.

"Fatima!" Mother cried, stepping nearer. "Fatima, I am so sorry. It took us some time to come, I know, but here we are. . ."

She tried to pull me with her, but I preferred to remain where I was.

But there was a time a few years back, when I greeted Fatima with friendliness and smiled at her. It was after Mother and I first arrived in Samarkand, after months on crowded refugee trains, and saw Fatima waiting in the entrance to the house to greet us. She was one of the few Uzbecks who had agreed to rent rooms to refugees. We had received her name and address scribbled on a piece of paper, at the train station.

It was winter. We were cold and frightened and did not know what was awaiting us at the end of the trek through yellow puddles on dark windy alleys. When she brought us up to the long dark room and left us there, I thought we would spend the night huddled together on the mattress in the corner. But she reappeared after a while. She carried a basket of coal in one hand, a tea pot in the other, and on her head she balanced a brass tray. It was loaded with fragrant pittas, raisins and nuts. We had been living on dry bread and thin soups for months. This looked like a miracle. She lit a fire in a small square pit in the middle of the room.

"Eat, drink, please!" She spoke Russian.

"Thank you." Mother pulled me to the fire and, her hand shivering, poured the tea into the small round cups.

"Handsome woman," she said to me in Polish. "God bless her!"

I did not think her wrinkled brown face was handsome, but I liked the smile in her dark, slightly slanted eyes and the huge silver amulet that hung from her neck on a heavy chain. I was also intrigued with the silver earrings made of small coins that dangled from her ears, and the embroidered hat on top of her head, two thick braids coiled around it. With her face reddish in the glow coming from the coals in the pit, she looked to me as if she had emerged from a fairy tale—a gypsy or a mysterious queen.

She still looked like a mysterious queen to me a few days later, when she took me to her house to show me how she baked her pittas. I watched her mix the dough, form it into flat pancakes, then squat in front of the fire like an ancient priestess. She threw the pancakes on the smoke-blackened wall of the oven and then sat and waited. With my legs drawn up beneath me I stared at her, at the fire, at the pancakes rising, then falling off the wall. She grabbed them and brushed the tops with a yellow mixture made of yolks. She made small pittas for me from the remnants she scraped off the walls of the container and engraved my name in the dough with her long, dark fingernail.

She had also once showed me her silver amulet. It had hinges and a minute door that opened to reveal a tiny scroll densely covered with letters. She said it guarded her from bad luck and diseases and also from the evil eye. It was supposed to ensure her a long life, prosperity and happiness in marriage.

A few weeks later I met her daughters, Savo Djon and Alua.

The first thought that occurred to me when I saw the two was how very little they resembled each other. Savo Djon was skinny and dark, her face long and nut-brown. Her almond-shaped eyes, set deeply in their sockets, stared at the world sadly and thoughtfully. Alua, the younger, was chubby and light-skinned and her cheeks were red. Her hair was black and shiny, like a well polished turtle-shell, and she tied to the ends of her braids small bells that tinkled as she walked.

When we were all older—when I was ten, Savo Djon fifteen, and Alua fourteen—I heard women in the street say that there were young men after Alua from the time she was twelve. "She is like a red apple," they said, "pink outside, inside sweet and white. No wonder the young men want to take a bite." But it looked as if no young men wanted to take a bite off Savo Djon, they said, unless they liked dry almonds, and there were not many such men around. And they laughed at their own smartness. But I felt offended, for I liked Savo Djon. She had taught me my first words in Russian and in Uzbeck and played with me often, though I was younger than she.

Savo Djon told me many legends of Samarkand. The one I liked best was about the beautiful princess who brought from her native land a small gray worm as a betrothal present. Though the worm lay in a golden box studded with precious stones, the people of Samarkand were offended, for they considered it an insult. Many merchants in the old bazaars wore their beards dishevelled, to demonstrate their sadness and confusion. But they combed their beards very soon after, for the princess placed the worm on a mulberry leaf and the worm spun the most beautiful white cocoon. She then taught them how to make the finest silk in the world, and the merchants had many reasons to rejoice, for the world came to their bazaars on camels, horses and donkeys and they became wealthy and famous. The women of Samarkand were the best dressed in the world, for even the poorest wore silks.

But Savo Djon's dress was not made of silk. It was made of dark cotton, its sleeves were too long and they partially covered her hands. It was Alua who had the silk dresses and velvet vests to go with them. When I asked her, she said she did not like silk dresses. It was hard for me to believe. She also said that Alua was going out more and needed them, while she preferred to stay home.

This was true. I never saw Savo Djon go with Alua and Fatima when the two went visiting or into town. They were a sight to behold then, for their dresses were long and colourful and their vests were embroidered with sequins. They wore square tibeteyka hats artfully embroidered with roses and leaves and had dainty slippers on their feet. Unlike other older women Fatima never wore a cape or a veil, and many years of balancing various things on her head made her carriage erect and proud. Savo Djon said she did not mind at all, that she liked being alone, and yet I thought that once I noticed some sadness in her eyes when she said goodbye to them at the door.

In my second or third year in Samarkand Savo Djon revealed to me that Fatima was not her real mother. I was taken aback. She was the first person I knew who had a stepmother. All my knowledge about stepmothers came from the few fairy tales I knew—"Cinderella," "Snow White" and "Hansel and Gretel." I looked at Savo Djon with pity.

"Don't you miss your real mother?" I asked.

"I never knew my real Mother," she said placidly, "so why should I miss her?"

"But what about Fatima?" I asked. "Is she the same to both of you?"

There was a slight tremor to her voice when she said: "Fatima is a good mother to me."

But I knew she lied and I started regarding Fatima the way one regards a strange and ferocious animal in the zoo. I thought about the differences between Alua and Savo Djon, I thought about the dresses. I remembered Savo Djon's sad eyes when the two were leaving her alone at home and I knew she was trying to conceal things from me. Soon I was to notice even more.

In my third year in Samarkand I started going to a school for refugees' children, where I had Polish and Jewish friends. Repeating what they heard from their parents they said the Uzbecks were "uncivilized" and "backward" and that we all lived in "wild Asia." When I asked my mother for the meaning of the words, she hesitated before answering. Then she said that it meant that people here had different customs and understood things differently from us. I was not satisfied with Mother's answer, for it did not explain the malicious expressions that appeared on my friends' faces when they said these words. I questioned Mother about it, but she would not respond.

In spite of what my school friends said, I liked Savo Djon and I liked Samenchuk. I continued playing with them when, in the summer, my other friends scattered away to other parts of the city where they lived.

In the beginning of the fourth summer, when I was nine years old, I noticed that I grew up almost as tall as Savo Djon, though she was fourteen. But then everyone said I was tall for my age. I also noticed that her skin became yellowish and all of a sudden she looked as if she had shrivelled. She told me she was sick with malaria in the winter. That was the year when Savo Djon quit school and started selling pittas in the square. I was surprised to see her there, but she said she had to, that Fatima needed help and money. And yet I knew well that Fatima was no poorer than her neighbours, that the women in the street treated her with deference not only on account of her age, and that Alua went to school. Savo Djon said Alua was the smarter one. I knew this too was untrue. Alua could not tell stories. Alua could not speak Russian. Savo Djon could.

I often watched her out in the square, where the pitta sellers competed for the street trade with vendors of grapes, figs and pumpkin seeds. They formed a group of their own beneath the largest mulberry tree and converged noisily on passersby, many of whom came on camels, donkeys and makeshift carts. But Savo Djon never mingled with the others. She stood apart from them and waited till a customer approached her.

It was also the summer when I first saw Savo Djon's room. I went to get some pittas from Fatima's bakery, in the rear of the house. The door to Savo Djon's room stood ajar. I peeked in. The room was small and dark and contained only a narrow bed and a wooden shelf on top of which was a kerosene burner and two bowls. It looked as if Savo Djon did her cooking there, for a strong smell of food and spices came out of the room. When I mentioned it to her, she was startled.

"How do you know I don't eat with the others?" she asked. I told her I saw the kerosene burner and the bowls.

"I eat different food than they... that's all," she retorted. But I saw she was uneasy about it and I knew that Fatima was to blame for it all.

One windy evening, Savo Djon's *tibeteyka* was blown away. During the short space of time when her head was uncovered I had noticed something very strange. Savo Djon had gray hair. Patches of gray hair covered her scalp. She put the *tibeteyka* on and ran away as if she were frightened. I knew that gray hair came from age or from worry, and Savo Djon was not old.

Then, one day she fainted and lay flat on the pavement. The pitta vendors scattered. Alua sprinkled Savo Djon's face with cold water from Suleiman's jug and she recovered. I was in the entrance to the house in the evening, when Old Suleiman came to ask for his payment. He brought the water from the springs up in the hills and sold it by the glass. Fatima became angry when he demanded payment for four glasses. She quarrelled with him noisily and called him a thief. He called her old witch. They settled for two pittas and Suleiman went away, cursing. I overheard the women in the street say that Savo Djon did not eat enough; they also said Fatima used to behave towards her differently when Savo Djon's father was around, before he went to the front, like my father.

It was then that I made up my mind to help Savo Djon. I thought I could write to her father. But where was he? Did he speak Russian? Then I decided to read to her the story of

Cinderella. Perhaps she would understand. Perhaps she would write and complain to her father. I had an old Polish book with colourful pictures and I brought it down to the square. She regarded the pictures with interest, then handed the book to me.

"Read, little one," she said gently.

I read slowly and distinctly, to make sure she understood. From time to time I lifted my eyes to examine her reactions, but she just stared at me out of her dark sad eyes. The sadness was still there when Cinderella put on the slipper and turned into a princess.

"Why are you sad, Savo Djon?" I asked. "The story ended well for Cinderella."

Savo Djon pondered my question for a while, then said, "I am sad for the stepmother and the stepsisters."

"What?!" I almost screamed. "Perhaps I should read it again?! Perhaps you did not understand?!"

"I understood well, little one. You read well and clearly."

I was proud but not happy. I felt I was shrinking a little under Savo Djon's gaze. "How can you, Savo Djon? They were bad and ugly and cruel to Cinderella!"

"That is why I am sorry for them, little one. Their hearts were full of hate and envy. Cinderella worked hard, but she was kind and healthy. And she married a prince. So why should I feel sorry for her?"

I knew I was failing somewhere. I did not know what to answer. The ground was slipping beneath my soles. I made a last, desperate effort.

"That means that you are also sorry for your stepmother and stepsister. They treat you like a servant. You are like Cinderella, Savo Djon! They wear nice dresses! They send you out to sell pittas in the street! You live in a dark room! You don't even eat with them!"

She did not answer. She just looked at me thoughtfully for a long time and I thought that I noticed tears in her eyes. She then said, "It's getting late, little one. I must go home."

I remained all by myself on the steps of the mosque. The neighs of camels settling for the night in some remote *caravanserai* came from a distance; a woman sang lullabyes to her baby on a balcony across the street.

I put the book under my arm and walked upstairs to our room, which was dim and cool like a mystery. I sat by the window. The clouds were now crimson. The nippled minarets and towers of Registan glistened in the distance. I opened the book and looked again at the picture of the stepsisters and the stepmother, trying to gather sympathy for them. But I could not. This is what they meant by the word "backward," I thought. They just cannot understand the simplest thing. Then I threw the book into the corner, the way one throws an item that has outlived its usefulness. Summer ended soon after and I went back to my winter friends from school.

The following summer—my fifth summer in Samarkand—Savo Djon and I grew closer. That was perhaps because I needed a friend more than ever. As Father's absence lengthened, Mother became more nervous and had less and less patience with me. She slapped me frequently and spent more time away from home. So I spent longer periods of time out in the square playing with Samenchuk, who was a liar, but fun to be with, watching Savo Djon sell her pittas and talking to her on the steps of the wooden mosque. It was nice to be spending those long free hours in the square. I liked the smells of spicy foods that wafted from the stalls, the colours and the sounds that surrounded us. When Mother's voice summoned me, I dragged my feet unwillingly up the stairs, then waited impatiently for the next day.

That fifth summer was unbearably hot. By the time the last days of August came, everyone wished an end to it. The cotton fields were in bloom earlier than usual. The tufts that floated in the air irritated children's eyes and they walked around looking as if they were crying. The last of the mulberries were ripening on the trees, sweet and mushy, perfect food for the thousands of silkworms that spun white cocoons on their leaves. The women in the street talked about a heavy winter coming and about some strange disease of the silkworm that was spreading, that might affect the cocoons and cause the butterflies to emerge deformed and die. Otherwise, things were the same.

On one of those days I came down to the square wearing new white shorts with a red butterfly sewn below my belly. Mother cut it out of an old pillow and stitched it on clumsily. Samenchuk gave a long whistle at the sight of me.

We were going to harvest the last of the mulberries and Samenchuk was ready with his white sheet, which he spread under the tree. Savo Djon was already there with her pittas and she smiled at me. She squatted in the shadow of the tree taking her midday rest. The pitta vendors in their colourful dresses and hats looked like a bunch of flowers laid on the yellow ground. Summer insects danced in the air and a group of butterflies whirled towards the women. Samenchuk climbed up the tree. He shook the branches and it started raining mulberries. The women picked them from between the folds of their dresses, laughing merrily and jokingly scolding the boy. He came down, tied the corners of the sheet together and carried the load to the other side of the street, where there was a wooden awning above a store entrance. We divided the loot between us, then squatted under the awning. The ripe mulberries melted as we ate them, their sweet nectar spilling from the corners of our mouths. Then we sat there silent and tired, watching the pitta vendors and chasing some lethargic flies from our legs.

Around noon time the street became very empty and quiet. People must have gone to find shelter from the heat in the cool interiors of their homes. Only the vendors remained, but even they were not as noisy as always. Old Suleiman sat in a shady corner and drank the spring water from his jug, a very unusual thing for him to do.

I noticed the woman in the dark cape right away. At first she looked like a long dark shadow. She came from the alley that led to the cemetery and approached the group of women in slow limping steps. They did not converge upon her the way they always did. They just sat there and stared.

Savo Djon was closest to the alley and the woman addressed her first. The girl rose to her feet; it was customary for a younger woman not to remain seated in the presence of an older one. The woman asked her to uncover the pittas, then pinched them one by one. She told Savo Djon to bring up the bottom one. She then lifted her veil. Her face was wrinkled and her eyes were very small. She unbuttoned her dress and brought out a dirty leather pouch. She took some coins out and counted them into Savo Djon's hand one by one. When she stopped I saw Savo Djon shaking her head. She was protesting something. The woman seemed angry. Suddenly her small eyes rested on Savo Djon's hand. She then lifted her head and examined the girl's face. Shrieking shrilly she took a step backwards. Savo Djon's eyes widened in fright. She retreated, the pittas falling to the ground and rolling away in the dust. The pitta vendors yelled, rising to their feet. In a minute they were gone. Savo Djon too disappeared into the entrance of the house.

It all happened very fast. Only Samenchuk, I and the old woman remained in the sunlit square. She stood there a while longer, then looking stealthily around gathered into her cape the pittas that rolled from Savo Djon's hands. She shouted something in Uzbeck and waved a clasped fist in the direction of the house, then scurried back to where she had come from. Only then did I ask Samenchuk for the meaning of it all. But he seemed angry and restless, then hurried away too. I remained all alone. I ran home, hoping to find out what had happened. But all was very quiet there too. Mother was away, at work. The carved door to the inner yard stared mutely at me. I climbed up on the veranda and pushed the wooden shutters that opened out into Fatima's garden. The garden was empty. Only some birds chirped faintly in the pomegranate trees and the open entrances to the house gaped at me, dark and mysterious. I went to our room then, closed the shutters and curled up on top of my mattress. Overcome by heat, I fell asleep.

I awoke to the sound of screams. It was dark outside. Mother had let me sleep through supper. I was hungry. At first I thought I was waking from a nightmare. *It's Savo Djon.* I sat on my bed and listened. The screams were coming from that direction. *She had lost the pittas and Fatima was punishing her. I hated Fatima!* I slid off the mattress and went to the other side of the room, where my mother was lying immobile on a low bed. In the light of the moon I could see that her eyes were wide open.

"Mother, what is it?" I whispered. "Has it been going on for a long time?"

"No, no, calm down."

She made me lie next to her and covered my ears with her hands. But I could hear.

"It's Savo Djon, Mother. I know. She lost her pittas today.

Did you know Fatima was not her real Mother? Yes, she is her stepmother and she will kill her . . . Call police, Mother. I'm afraid."

"The police station is far away. Besides we are strangers here. We do not know their customs."

Mother was afraid too. I could hear the shots of the falling whip. I wanted to scream too, but could not. It went on like this for a terrible while. Then the screams ceased as if cut by a knife. Terrible silence followed. Then there were loud knocks on the front gate. Mother and I rushed out and we saw a dishevelled Fatima running towards the gate with a lantern. Two policemen came in. They demanded to be admitted to the inner yard. And then her awful words: "She is dead, Comrade Commandant, there is nothing to search for. She is dead."

I stood leaning against the whitewashed wall of the yard. The woman in the blue cape brought in a tray with grapes and yellow figs which were artfully arranged on top of fresh green leaves. She then put some coals in the cavity of the small samovar. She laid it out on top of a low table with nacreous inlay and brought it to where Mother and Fatima were seated. Mother motioned to me to come nearer. Fatima looked at me, smiled and handed me a cup of tea. If she only knew what thoughts I harbored in my heart. We drank in silence. Fatima fingered the silver amulet on her chest, all the while looking to the ground. When we had finished drinking she lifted her head and cast a hazy glance around her.

"It's a heavy loss for us all," she said.

Mother nodded and I looked at Fatima hatefully.

"I loved her like my own daughter," she said.

Mother bowed her head low and I had a sudden urge to run away and never set my eyes on Fatima again. She must have noticed our silence and reticence, for she sat staring sadly ahead, her fingers clasped around the amulet. Then, stuttering slightly, as if trying to overcome a strong hesitation, she began talking again.

"Madame Solomonovna," she said, turning her eyes upon Mother, "when I married her father, Savo Djon was only a tiny baby. Alua was born very soon after, so I could still nurse Savo

73

Djon for a while. So you see," she said with a tiny smile, as if the memory was a pleasant one for her, "sometimes they both sucked at the same time, each at one breast."

Mother just sat there silently, her hands clasped in her lap, the fringes of her black shawl touching the ground. She turned towards me as if she looked in my face for answers, but I had none. What Fatima was saying made everything for me so much less comprehensible. Fatima must have understood, for she said, half sadly, half angrily: "You must have harsh thoughts about me, Madame Solomonovna."

Mother started pulling nervously on the corners of the shawl. "Well," she said finally, "you know . . . we heard Savo Djon's screams that night, then we saw the police . . . and also people talk . . ."

"Yes, yes, I understand." Fatima nodded sadly.

I looked at her and all of a sudden she was only a sad old woman, so different from a mysterious queen in a tale. As if sensing the change in me she took my hand and pulled me towards her. She held my head in her lap and I hid my face in the folds of her robe. She smelled of balsam and of soft warm silk. When she started talking again I got up. She told Mother then how lucky she was to have such a smart and healthy girl. Mother answered that she was indeed. Fatima then said that she too was lucky in having at least one healthy girl.

"We did not know Savo Djon was sick," Mother said after a pause. "She never missed a day out in the square."

Fatima lifted her head. Quietly, as if afraid to be overheard she said, "Madame Solomonovna, do you know what leprosy is?"

Mother nodded.

"Savo Djon was a leper."

"What?!" Mother's eyes widened and she just sat there rigid like a sculpture. "Little Savo Djon . . . a . . . leper?"

We talked about it at school once. The teacher said there were some sicknesses here, in the Orient, that were extinct where we came from. She mentioned cholera and leprosy and said cholera was not the worst, for one died fast. About leprosy she said some things that were too frightening to think about.

"I knew about it for five years," Fatima went on. "I have prayed to Allah for enlightenment. I also visited a few of our old healers and wise men. They told me it was not as contagious as people believed if one kept clean and took in certain spices and herbs. But the Russian authorities think differently. So I decided to hide her. You know, Madame Solomonovna, what would have been the alternative?!"

I watched Mother. She knew.

"Yes," she said with an expression of horror on her face, "Yes, I know . . . a leper colony."

"A leper colony in the desert!" cried Fatima. "Where they live like animals, worse than animals, their limbs falling one by one, their faces a rotting wound, till they die, their bones scattered on the rocks. Could you do it to your child, Madame Solomonovna?! Could you?!"

A shiver ran through Mother as she looked at me. Her lips curved down unhappily and there were tears in her eyes. I started crying. The woman in the blue cape brought white cloth and rose water to wash our faces. Fatima dropped her hands into her lap in a gesture of helplessness and fatigue.

"For five long years I managed to keep it a secret. Believe me, Madame Solomonovna, it was not easy. We lived in constant fear. I had to engage her in the selling of pittas to keep her out of school and protect her from being forced to work in cotton fields. Otherwise there was no need for her to work."

I squatted on the edge of the wooden platform. So it was all different from what I thought. Fatima motioned to the woman in blue and she refilled our cups.

"Satan himself," Fatima cried clasping her amulet, "Satan in person must have sent the accursed woman to our street that day. She used to work with lepers. She saw what others did not. She threatened to notify the authorities. May she hang by her tongue! There are severe penalties imposed for hiding a leper."

My mother raised her eyebrows questioningly.

"There were not many choices left, Madame Solomonovna," Fatima sighed. We knew the police would be here before dawn. So we agreed, she and I, that I should beat her till she bled . . . That way they were not going to touch her. That's what I told her . . . that they won't touch a bleeding leper . . . Savo Djon tried not to scream . . ." Fatima started sobbing uncontrollably. I was scared. The woman in blue rushed to her side, but she waved her away.

"Savo Djon tried not to scream," she sobbed. "But it was too painful. Believe me, Madame Solomonovna . . . my heart bled with every shot of the whip." She buried her head in her hands. My mother looked bewildered. I just squatted there, numb, not knowing what to do. I looked beyond Fatima's head. The pomegranates on the tree were ripe and red and deep shadows lay in the small arbour of vines. The sky was very clear and the woman in blue stood in the entrance to the house watching us all respectfully.

Then I saw Mother leaning towards Fatima and I heard her whispering, "But Fatima, dear Fatima, did it not occur to you that she might die of the beating?"

Fatima straightened her back and looked into Mother's eyes, her head held up proudly.

"Madame Solomonovna!" she said. There was a note of disappointment in her tone. "Madame Solomonovna, I know you are a learned and intelligent woman . . . and yet, yet you do not seem to understand . . . " She paused and looked at me. I knew she would have preferred I was not there. Then, leaning very close to Mother, her face tense and almost cruel, she whispered hoarsely, "Do you really think a leper colony in the desert would have been better?!"

Crickets started chattering somewhere in the grass. My mother lifted her hand to her lips.

Fatima got up, like a queen at the end of an audience. My mother rose to her feet too. The woman in blue stood erect, then bowed deeply.

I knew then it was time for us to leave.

THE VISITOR FROM ESTONIA

On that sunny June day I woke up earlier than usual. The bedroom, which I shared with my parents, was empty. The bed was not made and its white percale sheets were shining against the mahogany headboard. The heavy feather pillows still bore deep imprints of two heads. The windows were open and only partly covered by the gray macramé curtains. Small fragments of rainbows danced on the wall and the floor was a mosaic of shadows and lights.

I slid off the bed, and approached the window barefoot. It opened on a long narrow yard surrounded by the flat dirty facades of three buildings. The yard was paved with dark cement and decorated with chalk-drawn designs, letters and numbers.

A woman rolled a carpet out of an open window. Balconies were loaded with piles of bedding brought out for an airing. The radio in the apartment just above ours was playing a languid tango:

> *When in all the city gardens*
> *The lillies bloom,*
> *Then again my dear beloved*

I'll see you in
My room!

The buildings still bore traces of war. There was a bullet hole in the wall across from ours, many windows were still patched with strips of paper, an awning was hanging on exposed metal rods. But children were playing ball and hopscotch, and mothers were pushing prams to the sunny end of the yard, where a few freshly painted green benches waited for them.

I yawned and stretched and contemplated with pleasure the two months of vacation ahead, long and carefree. Then I saw my friend Halina, her blond hair shining in the sun, playing hopscotch. "Halina!" I called. "Halina!" but she did not hear.

I was about to get dressed and go down to see her when my eyes fell again on the two pillows. Why was the second pillow creased? Father was away. All of a sudden I remembered. Aunt Marysia was here! She was supposed to arrive on a night train. I opened the closet and there were her suitcase and a few neatly wrapped boxes. *Presents!* Aunt Marysia was here and I was wasting my time looking out of windows! I ran towards the door that opened onto a long corridor that led to the kitchen.

I wanted to surprise her, so I walked on my tiptoes. But I stopped in the middle of the long stretch because I heard two voices coming from the kitchen. The voices were laughing and giggling. This would not have been unusual at all if one of them, the louder and the merrier, had not belonged to my mother.

I was eleven years old then. My memories from that time are quite clear, like photos taken with a good camera. If I could, I would have arranged them in a picture album, one of the heavy, leather-bound ones, with dark pages and with sticky cellophane corners to tuck the photos into. There would have been five pictures inserted into the album on the day the man from Estonia came for a visit: my father's, my mother's, Aunt Marysia's, mine and, of course, the visitor's.

Father's image would be small, as if taken from a distance. He would be smiling his gentle, slightly pained, almost absent smile. My father was an artist, a painter. But he gave up painting so that he could earn enough to support us. Mother always needed more than he earned. His lips are curved down, which gives his face an expression of disappointment. He is standing in front of an iron gate behind which there stands a large-windowed factory building. He was the manager of a government-operated factory for recycling. Instead of painting, he taught people how to sort out rags so that they were fit to be used in the production of paper.

He was frequently sent to branches of the company in remote villages and town. He seemed to like those assignments. When he was home Mother and he quarrelled frequently and loudly. Sometimes, enraged, he paced the floor, his head clutched between his hands, then he would put his coat on, slam the door and leave. He would return late in the evening, drunk and wobbly on his feet, hum a song sadly, smile faintly and apologetically at me, then fall on the bed and snore loudly.

On the day of the visit he was away on assignment. His picture would be in light browns, like the colour of his eyes.

My picture would be the next one. It would be bluish-gray, the colour of the second hand, "best" dress I was wearing that day. My eyes are grayish-blue too. They stare at the world with curiosity and liveliness. I wear braids with two large white ribbons that look like birds perched on my shoulders. I stand next to my doll house. It is white, has a red roof, red door and red shutters and a little garden is painted on its wall. I liked this doll house very much. I spent every spare penny to buy furniture and small dolls whose eyes opened and closed. During the war, when I was in Russia, I had no toys. I knew they existed from stories told by my parents but I never saw a doll before I was nine years old.

During the war we played all kinds of games for which we did not need toys. We played "soldiers" and we fought mock battles. We also played "traitor." There was a final ceremony when we hung the traitor who pretended to be dead by sticking his tongue out and rolling his eyes.

When I returned to Poland, Aunt Marysia presented me with the doll house. Father had installed electricity in it and my little doll-family of mother, father and three daughters lived there a harmonious and pleasant life in a luxurious two bedroom apartment, enjoying comforts I never knew. My dolls never played "traitor" and "soldier."

Aunt Marysia's picture would be the next one. It is in bright colours, large and very clear. She was not a real aunt. After the war all my parents' friends had become "aunts" and "uncles." My real aunts and uncles had all been killed during the war, in bombing raids and in concentration camps. Aunt Marysia was Jewish too, but her husband was a Pole and he saved her and their son, Yanek. They lived in a small old town on the shores of the river Vistula, and it was in their home that I spent my first Christmas in Poland and saw my first Christmas tree. They were very loving to each other and I watched with envy when Aunt Marysia kissed her son.

Aunt Marysia had an olive complexion, brown hair, and two lovely dimples formed on her face whenever she smiled. She smiled almost constantly. Her teeth were white and even. She used to say that her dimples and her teeth were her dowry. I wondered about the charming little black spot just beneath her lip. Was that part of her dowry too? She told me it was not, that it was not real; she bought it at the pharmacy for five zloty. I decided to buy a black spot like hers when I grew up and was sorry dimples were not for sale as well.

When it came to sewing, nobody I knew could equal Aunt Marysia. She would make scraps of material into beautiful skirts and kerchiefs, artfully sew together little pieces of felt into dainty purses and muffs, cut remnants in such a way that they would suffice to make a skirt or a blouse. After each of her visits I had a few of them hanging in the closet. She always wore wide colourful skirts and bright blouses that revealed her smooth, dark shoulders.

Mother's picture would be in black and white, square, its edges slightly yellowed. Her face is sharp and distinct, her features stern and unforgiving. The face is not very old, but it is prematurely wrinkled, particularly around the eyes and around the corners of her lips. Her lips curve down and give her face an expression of bitterness. Her nose is straight, sharp and determined and her eyes are very light iron gray. Mother seemed to have suspended a heavy curtain between herself and my father and I, and she never told me about her past. The only time when the curtain ever opened was on that June day, a few hours after

I stood in the dim corridor and, surprised, listened to her laugh.

"After such a long time," I heard Aunt Marysia's voice. "How does that make you feel?"

Mother answered something in a low voice, then started laughing again. I stood there motionless, uneasy, with some fear in my heart. The usual barrage of complaints and remarks was somehow safer than this laughter. I advanced cautiously towards the kitchen door. When the two became silent, I knocked. Aunt Marysia opened the door and a moment later I was in her arms, laughing and covering her face with kisses.

"Why didn't you wake me up when you came?" I cried. "I was looking forward to seeing you for such a long time! Will you stay long?" I was hanging on her neck, embracing her and pulling her towards me. She seated me on the kitchen counter, then stepped back to have a better look at me.

"Have we not grown up from the time I last saw you!"

Her face was lit by a wide, radiant smile. I smiled back at her. I felt tall all of a sudden and I straightened my back to appear even taller.

"You must have outgrown all your clothes!" she exclaimed. "But don't worry! Aunt Marysia can do something about it! Right, Mother?"

I turned to look at Mother. She was observing the scene without a word. Instead of scolding me, as usual, about my bare feet, dishevelled hair, or the way I was standing, she just stood there smiling. She looked as if she was not even seeing us, or the ladle in her hand.

There were millions of things on my mind to ask Aunt Marysia about and I turned back to her. I asked about Yanek and Uncle Ted and the skating on the Vistula, and the repairs to the old church. Aunt Marysia laughed at the barrage of questions and told me she could not answer them all. She could not answer them, she said, because she had no time today. Saying this, she stressed the word "today" in a particular way, then turned towards Mother as if asking her permission to continue. Mother looked away distractedly.

Aunt Marysia looked at me as if she was weighing something in her mind, then uttered slowly and guardedly: "You see, love, we shall be busy today, Mother and I. You see . . . we are

81

expecting a visitor, a very important visitor."

There was a look of slight embarrassment on her face. She sighed and fretted and turned her eyes away. I had never seen her this way.

"What visitor?" I asked alarmed. "I thought you were our most important visitor."

"Of course I am," she said. "But tonight there will be someone else coming. He is coming from far away, from Estonia. He is coming to see your mother."

There was something in her tone that made me feel uneasy, and I opened my eyes wide. Estonia sounded strange and remote.

"Is he someone from our family?"

"No, just a friend. An old, old friend."

"How old is this old friend, Aunt Marysia?"

"Not so very old. He is not wrinkled or bearded or leaning on a cane. An old friend is a friend from long ago, someone one has known for a long time."

I glanced towards Mother. She was still standing there with a ladle in her hand. She looked at us, but did not see us. Her expression was so much softer than usual. She was smiling. I asked her whether she knew the friend from the time they were children and she turned to me and absentmindedly answered that she did not. Then, hesitantly and stiffly, as if she did not want to discuss the subject with me, she added that she knew him from much later.

I wanted to know more, but Aunt Marysia said I was too curious and curious children became old and wrinkled fast. She then slapped me lightly and pushed a list of groceries into my hand. It was for our grocer, Mr. Kuba. She told me to get dressed fast, that there were some errands waiting for me. I went into the bedroom and when I returned Mother and Aunt Marysia were talking to each other in low voices.

"Don't be silly," Aunt Marysia said, "You don't look old at all."

"But I'm embarrassed," Mother answered. "I was young and pretty then."

"Don't forget that he has not become younger himself . . . "

I made a noisy entrance to the kitchen. Mother gave me some

instructions and I sauntered down the corridor and the two flights of stairs.

In the yard I stopped to exchange a few words with Halina, then hopped towards the gate, all the while turning the shopping net above my head. Then through the heavy gate and out into the wide central street. Mother's unusual behavior, the suddenness and unexpectedness of the visit, the hushed atmosphere, confused and worried me.

I stopped in front of the window of a toy shop. A large yellow chick stared at me from the top of a square box, but it did not have any answers for me. I glanced at the grocery list in my hand. It was much longer than usual and included written instructions for Mr. Kuba. Words like "best," "choicest," "softest" and "freshest" were added to all but the canned items and even those bore elaborations like "the bigger one" and "imported."

I handed the note to Mr. Kuba. I noticed he had an air of satisfaction on his face when he summed up the purchases. They were heavy to carry and it took me a while to get back home. When I entered, I could not recognize the apartment. Chairs were standing on the table; curtains were gathered to the side of the window; carpets, rolled and tied with strings, leaned on each other in the corner. Mother, Aunt Marysia and the janitor's wife, wearing kerchiefs and holding feather dusters, were engaged in an orgy of cleaning.

Sun now burst unashamedly through the bare windows and clouds of dust whirled around. The severe sculptured figures on our heavy credenza were being polished and shined, their smiles visible again. Layers of dust were being swiftly wiped from their hats and from within the sculpted folds of their brown mahogany robes. The chandelier burst into a merry peal of clinking, its pointy crystals sparkling and shimmering. The white tiles of the corner stove shone after the energetic rubbing they were given by the janitor's wife, and the sofa, spread lazily on its low, curved legs, displayed its pale velvety covers, clean and mended. In the midst of it all the three moved swiftly, pointing to corners, moving books and magazines, shining vases and silver dishes, dipping figurines into bowls of soapy water, then taking them out, all bubbly and irridescent, and laying them down on soft flannel cloths.

At noon the room sparkled and smelled of wax. Edges of heavily hanging curtains softly caressed the carpets, admitting rays of sun through their thickly crocheted nets. Shadows concealed the rubbed-off corners of the upholstered chairs. The damask tablecloth bore patiently the old wine stains that resisted hand washing and detergents. Some of the stains were concealed under the white porcelain dishes bordered with gold, another remnant of someone's "good old days." A silver tea set, borrowed from the upstairs neighbours, decorated the top of the credenza, bringing with it the charm of long-forgotten opulence. Violets in small vases drew attention away from the modest imitation-crystal wine glasses. It all looked splendid, so splendid that it almost made me forget the uneasiness and suspicion I had carried within me since the morning.

Aunt Marysia opened the door quietly and stood next to me. "Isn't it lovely?" she whispered. "Your Mother has that special touch when it comes to decorating. I still remember the party she arranged for me before the war in your parents' country house. People talked about it for years afterwards." I wanted to tell her I knew nothing about it, that it was the first time for me, but her eyes sparkled with such genuine delight that I kept quiet. She pushed me towards the bedroom.

"Go, take a nap now, then get dressed nicely."

I did not feel like taking a nap. There was too much going on, there were too many things happening in my life: the royally set table; Mother smiling and obviously happy; Aunt Marysia; the visitor. This, I decided, was not a day to be wasted on afternoon naps. The yard beckoned to me, warm and noisy. Halina would probably still be there and I could share with her part of my excitement. I sneaked past the entrance hall and out into the bright yard. The games were going on as on other summer days with their rhythmic movements and subdued noises. I was surprised that nobody paid any special attention to me, that nobody was aware of the importance of what was happening in my life. I felt all of a sudden a great pity for them all playing their silly games. They did not know what life was all about, they did not have visitors coming unexpectedly out of mysterious-sounding Estonia, they did not have a sparkling table set on a weekday as if it were a holiday, and they could not appreciate or see the magic change that had occurred in our modest apartment since the morning.

I ran towards Halina. I told her all in one breath. Unperturbed, she went on throwing five pebbles up in the air, then gathering them with a swift motion of her hand.

"Big deal," she said when I had finished my story. "Want to play pebbles?"

I squatted next to her and threw the pebbles up. But I was not as fast as usual and they kept scattering and escaping to all sides. The afternoon was maturing slowly, and the shadows were becoming darker and longer. Men carrying small lunch boxes and thermoses were crossing the yard and disappearing into the dark narrow entrances. Smells of cooked food filled the air and mothers summoned children to come up. Radios were tuned to news broadcasts. The houses seemed to be leaning towards each other, exchanging gossip from balconies and open windows. Geraniums were very red on a few of the window sills, diapers and underwear fluttered in the air, white, pink and blue. Outside, pipes gurgled and spattered and the door of the small outhouse at the end of the yard squeaked shrilly, as if complaining about its unpleasant function. It was time for me to go home.

I ran up the stairs and opened the door. The apartment was dim and smelled clean and of fresh bread. Usually I would come in with a small fear in my heart, ready to defend myself against Mother's scathing remarks about my appearance and manners. But I had no fear today. Perhaps, I thought, things will be different from now on.

I opened the door to the living room. The table looked as splendid as before, though now it had the added allure of the semi-darkness. The whole room was festive and smelled of violets. Feminine voices, shrill and excited, reached me from the bedroom. I knocked on the door and entered. The bedroom was a mess. Petticoats, brassieres, dresses and skirts were spread around in disarray.

"Where were you all this time? We thought you were taking a nap." Mother's voice was unusually soft.

The only "good" dress I had was prepared for me on the bed. It was made of faded light imitation silk with white polka-dots. There was a small bouquet of coloured ribbon roses pinned to the front to conceal a button-hole out of place. It used to be someone else's dress. Aunt Marysia had converted it to fit me, but somehow had not managed to conceal the hole.

Mother took a dress I had never seen before out of the closet. It was black, was cut low in the back and had inserts of dark lace. The dress was sleeveless. Mother put it on, and for the first time I noticed that she had very smooth, white, shapely shoulders. They were completely exposed now. I was embarrassed to see her like this but had to admit it did look nice. My little faded dress appeared even paler by comparison. Mother glanced at herself in the mirror. She lifted her hand and smoothed her hair with the tips of her fingers, then tilted her head slightly and smiled at the reflection. Aunt Marysia leaned backwards with her hands on her hips.

"Look at that! Like a bride! So help me God!"

She made Mother's face up with swift, agile movements of her long fingers. The bluish-gray of Mother's eyes deepened, her eyelashes became dark and longer than before, and the streaks of gray in her eyebrows disappeared. The wrinkles seemed to disappear too under layers of cream, powder and rouge. Was this really my mother? Aunt Marysia, fussing with the pots of cream and powder and running around smoothing pleats and creases, brushing off some lint here, a speck of dust there, looked like a good fairy from "Cinderella."

Aunt Marysia herself put on a flowered skirt, a white blouse gathered with a ribbon around her shoulders and a handkerchief that matched the skirt. She needed no makeup.

The three of us went to the living room and sat down stiffly on the faded sofa. I glanced at Mother out of the corner of my eye. She was more serious now and, it seemed to me, slightly more nervous. From time to time she glanced at herself in a mirror suspended above the credenza and stroked back a wisp of hair from her forehead. We did not talk, each of us absorbed in her own thoughts.

"It's almost eight," Mother said, glancing at her watch. "He must be coming to the train station."

It was very quiet. Evening descended upon the yard, hiding the ugliness of the old buildings. Lights had come on in the windows across from ours. The lights were small and came from bare low-voltage bulbs. Curtains similar to ours, hand crocheted and heavy, hung in some of the windows. On other nights, I would stand patiently, trying to peek into neighbours' lives and weave stories around them. But today I had no time for that.

There was a sharp ring at the door. Mother rose quickly. She ran towards the door. Aunt Marysia followed her. I got up too, and approached the living room door, peeking curiously into the dim corridor. By now the entrance door was closed and Mother was standing next to it, facing a tall slim man in a dark brown suit.

"It's you, Volodya?" she exclaimed in Russian. He was quiet for a moment, than said softly, "Yes, it's me."

Then he gathered Mother into his arms. She was shorter than he and had to raise her head to see him. He kissed her hair, then pushed her gently away to look at her again, then gathered her into his arms again. *"Dorogaya moya !"* he said, "My dear!"

Mother took his arm and led him towards Aunt Marysia, who was standing in the middle of the corridor. "Please make the acquaintance of my dear friend, Marya Pavlovna, from the town of Plotsk."

"Most pleased and honoured to make your acquaintance on this pleasant occasion, Marya Pavlovna." He bent above her hand and kissed it gallantly. They all advanced towards me now, Mother holding the arm of the stranger. I have never seen her holding Father's arm this way.

"My little girl," she said. "She is eleven."

"A little girl," he said pensively, caressing my hair. "I did not know . . . you did not write . . . I always wanted a little girl."

Mother blushed. She led him into the room, looking at him shyly, awkwardly.

"Please, come in, feel at home. It's all so modest, after the war, you know . . . used to be different."

He looked around. "What are you talking about? Such splendour! And all this in my horour? I am not worthy, I assure you, my dear."

They looked at each other again, now in the bright full light of the living room chandelier, as if trying to absorb and sum up in seconds the changes that the years had wrought upon their faces.

"You have not changed much . . . " he said in a slightly shivering voice. "The same beautiful eyes." He took both her hands in his and kissed them. "It wasn't easy, the war, ah?" He was noticing the wrinkles and the shadows under Mother's eyes. As if not wanting him to see more, she averted her face.

He was not in the prime of youth either. His face looked tired. There was a deep scar on his cheek, and one of his fingers was missing. I looked at his hand questioningly.

"Frostbitten," he said. "In Siberia." He must have noticed my curious, searching look. Mother smiled at him, then put her hand on his shoulder.

"A tiny glass of vodka, Volodya?"

He smiled back at her. "Of course, my dear. We shall drink to the good old times and to the good old times to come!" He looked at Mother again and patted her hand, which stayed on his shoulder.

"You are still beautiful, my dear, still very very beautiful." Mother was radiant. I had never heard Father calling her beautiful, and I never thought she was, but tonight she looked different.

She left the room and a moment later returned carrying a small round tray in the middle of which a crystal carafe, also on loan from the neighbours, was surrounded by small vodka glasses. She poured a little vodka for each of them. They raised and clicked the glasses, then silently gulped the white liquid.

A slight shiver ran through the man's shoulders. He placed the glass on a tray. "Another one of those, my dear, please. They say that when one drinks a glass of vodka one becomes a different person. And a different person needs a glass of vodka too."

They laughed at the joke, then became silent again, as if some memories and impressions weighed heavily on their minds. Volodya opened a silver cigarette case and offered a cigarette to Aunt Marysia, then to Mother. They declined and he lighted one himself. The smoke created a mist around the three of them and they seemed to be closed in a little world I was not a part of.

I looked at Volodya. I liked him. He was a handsome man. He had a straight thin nose, light combed hair and bright intelligent eyes. He spoke Russian the way teachers and doctors in Russia spoke, softly and quietly, using long, beautiful words

and with the kind of inflection I always tried to imitate. He used
the diminutive form often and the words sounded as if they came
from somewhere deep within him. But in spite of all this there
was something that disturbed and irritated me about him. All
of a sudden I wished Father was here. All of a sudden it seemed
strange all this was going on when he was away. *They should
have waited with the dinner for him.*

Mother, in the meantime, arranged the appetizers on the
table. A pickled herring swam in a sea of marinated onions, and
red-capped mushrooms made of eggs and tomatoes surrounded
a green hill of vegetable salad, while in the neighbouring platter
ducks made of eggs and shaved radishes floated in a red lake of
tomato sauce. It all looked charming and summery and the guest
was expressing his wonder with loud "Ohs" and "Ahs". He was
seated at the head of the long table. Mother was very close to
him, on the left, Aunt Marysia on the right, and I was seated at
the other end of the table, across from him and at some distance
from everyone else.

The janitor's wife had been engaged to do the serving. She
was wearing a white kerchief that fell sharply over her left eye.
Without the mane of hair to draw attention away from it, her
nose looked even more prominent than before. It was so long that
I wondered whether she ever managed to kiss anyone without
the nose being in the way. The small white heart that formed the
upper part of her apron folded into the crevice between her
breasts, in spite of her efforts to stretch it on top of them with the
help of two safety pins.

Volodya smiled a wide smile at the sight of her

"*Karasavitsa!*" he whispered to Mother. "What a beauty!"

The janitor's wife went out and returned with a tureen of
soup. She ladled the soup slowly and carefully onto Volodya's
plate under his attentive gaze.

"Delicious soup, my dear." He turned to Mother. "Reminds
me of the one we used to eat in your little room." He lifted
Mother's hand to his lips, kissed it, then held it in his for a while,
looking into her eyes. Mother became dreamy and pensive and
smiled at him shyly. Then she noticed I was watching them and
quickly withdrew her hand.

"Those were the days," continued the visitor, undisturbed.

"We were poor, almost starving, but what spirit . . . "

The janitor's wife appeared again, carrying a large platter of cooked tongue with breaded Brussel sprouts. Mother must have been up early in the morning to prepare such elaborate displays. I could not remember a meal like this in our house since we had returned to Poland two years before. Why could we not have any of this before? I could hardly swallow.

The visitor, though, seemed to be enjoying himself very much. He was talking with animation, enjoying his food and refilling his vodka frequently. He was complimenting Mother profusely all the way. She in turn was beaming and piling food on his plate.

"Delicious, everything's just delicious. Your husband must consider himself a lucky man."

I almost choked on a shaved radish that I had been holding in my mouth for a while. I remembered with a tinge of bitterness the thin soups and the dry legs of chicken that were our daily fare.

Aunt Marysia watched Mother with a small conspirator's smile. Her large green and red kerchief fell to the arm of her chair, revealing her bronzed shoulders. Her hair descended on the nape of her neck in soft curls, and her eyes, enlivened by talk and alcohol, sparkled. She was nudging Mother discreetly with her elbow and Mother responded with a girlish smile. I had sent the remains of my food to the kitchen and just sat there, concealed by a large bottle of wine. It looked as if Mother had forgotten about me. But at that moment she threw a quick glance at me, then at her watch.

"It's too late for you to be sitting with the adults at the table. We will bring you your dessert in your bedroom."

I knew arguing would be useless, so I dejectedly got up and, curtsying politely to everyone, went to my room. Before closing the door I cast a last glance at the living room. The visitor was sitting with his back to me now, but I could see mother well. She was looking at him with a tenderness I had never seen in her eyes before, a tenderness I had never suspected her of having. Her hand was on his again and it seemed to me she was caressing it. I closed the door behind me and threw myself on the bed. From the living room there came the noise of clinking glasses, of laughing and the smell of cigarettes. I undressed and crawled under the blanket.

Some time later the door opened. In the lighted rectangle I saw the silhouette of a man. I thought for a minute Father had come back and I sat up on my bed, all ready to hug him. A moment after this, there was a click of the light switch and the room became bright.

Volodya was standing in front of the closed door. He held a small plate in his hand.

"The ladies are busy washing dishes," he said, "so I took it upon myself to bring you your dessert." He placed the small plate with a piece of cake on it on my night table, then pulled a chair close to my bed and sat facing me. Resentful as I was I could not dislike him completely. There was something nice about him. There was some sadness in his deep brown eyes, a little like the eyes of my Father, and a hint of some childishness in his clumsy movements and the way he sat there looking at me.

"You know," he said suddenly, "I once loved you mother very much." He said it so simply and with so much feeling that I was touched and startled. He leaned back in his chair, folded his arms, and his eyes wandered around the room, then returned to me. I asked him, hesitantly, where he met my mother. "We studied together for four years ... " he said. "Four long beautiful years in Paris. You don't know, little one, what it means to be young, to be in love and to be in Paris at the same time. One never forgets that. I hope you find out, though they say Paris is not what it used to be. But then nothing is the way it used to be. We went on trips together, visited museums or just walked on the banks of the river. It was beautiful."

He looked towards the open window as if expecting some more memories to float from the dark yard. But only a dark moth whirled in and started dancing furiously around the naked bulb. Turning to me again Volodya said very quickly, "But it all ended one day." The moth kept hitting the surface of the bulb.

"We received our degrees, you see. We had some plans to spend the summer together, then decide on our future. We knew we belonged together." He stopped and looked at me questioningly. "Your Mother never talked about it? You never heard about us?"

"No, I did not."

He looked surprised and glanced sideways as if weighing whether he should be the one to tell me. Then, placing his elbow on top of my night table he said: "Perhaps I shoud tell you, then. You see . . . something happened then. A telegram arrived. It was from Estonia, from my father, who was very ill. I had to leave right away. I promised to write. But there were complications in the family and I never did. I had hoped that your mother would understand, and wait. She did. For three months. I should have written, I know. It was all my fault. But we are such fools when we are young. And then, maybe there is the hand of fate in it all." He paused and looked at me anxiously as if afraid he was telling me things I could not understand. But I listened with interest and he went on.

"You see, she waited for three long months, alone in Paris. She had nothing more to do there and she was running out of funds, so one day she packed her valises and took the train to Poland. I arrived the next day. I ran up the stairs and knocked on the door. Only silence greeted me. I ran down to the concierge, still hoping. But I knew. You know, when you knock on a door of an empty or uninhabited apartment, it has a different sound. The concierge only could reaffirm what I feared most. She had left, she said, the day before, crying. I sat on the stairs and cried too. I did not even know where to look for her . . . I did not know her address in Poland . . . I had not seen her till today."

He stopped talking. His face was very sad. I tried to imagine Mother then. The concierge had said that she was crying. I had never seen Mother crying. She got angry and she shouted, but she never cried. I wondered if she had been a different person from the one I knew and feared, whether the world in which she lived was different and whether she was kinder and happier then.

Volodya put his hand on mine. "You are a nice girl," he said. "You could have been my daughter."

I looked at him, startled, and did not answer for a long moment. Then, as kindly and decisively as I could, I said, "No, it would have been a completely different girl. I am my father's daughter. I know, because my father's eyes are brown. And although mine are blue, like those of my mother, half of the left eye is brown, like his."

He smiled. "Still, you are a nice girl, and I wish you were mine.

"Still, I am my father's girl," I repeated.

He withdrew his hand rapidly and stared at me with a strange, pained expression. Perhaps he had just then realized that he was in another man's house, kissing another man's wife and talking to another man's daughter. Then he turned away from me and stared intently at the corner, where the walls met the ceiling. There was a small plaster cherub there, surrounded by garlands of plaster flowers and thickly covered with layers of paint. I looked at Volodya, at his sharp, handsome profile, at the scar on his cheek, at the forehead furrowed by wrinkles, and I felt sorry for him

"You may still have a little girl of your own," I said.

"I don't know," he said. "I don't know."

He then left the bedroom, closing the door gently. Then I heard him saying goodbye to Aunt Marysia. Both she and Mother were loudly protesting his short visit, the sudden and hasty departure. They urged him to stay longer.

"But Volodya," I heard Mother's voice "I . . . I was hoping you'd stay overnight with us."

There was a long silence afterwards. I heard the steps of the three in the corridor. The entrance door closed softly and Aunt Marysia came back to the living room. She started collecting the remaining dishes from the table. I heard Mother's and Volodya's loud steps and quiet voices in the yard below. I stood by the window. The moon was full and bright and the yard was purplish gray. I could distinguish the shape of Mother's white shoulders hugged by Volodya's arm. They stopped in the middle of the yard, and I saw Volodya kissing Mother for a long time. Then they walked towards the gate. A few minutes later I heard Mother coming in. She and Aunt Marysia continued whispering late into the night.

I tried to fall asleep then, but could not. I kept turning and tossing in my bed. Pictures from war time kept popping into my mind. I remembered how father got lost once and then reappeared, running in the field, his silhouette standing out against the setting sun. I remembered how he picked me up and then put his arm around Mother's shoulders. I remembered how we hid in a farmer's cottage till someone denounced us and how we ran away in the middle of the night and travelled on dark roads full of frightening shapes and threatening noises. I remembered the games we played and the horrible sight of the face with the tongue sticking out. I fell asleep only after Mother and Aunt Marysia came tiptoeing into the bedroom and settled in the large bed.

When I woke up the next morning, the sky was cloudy. The room looked cold and gray. I curled under the blanket. Mother and Aunt Marysia were in the living room and I could hear their voices clearly.

Then Mother entered the room. She was wearing her everyday dress and her hair was gathered into a bun. Her eyes were grayish and sad and her face looked drawn and tired. But there lingered some of yesterday's softness in her movements, and her voice was so much more subdued. She sat on my bed and stared at me for a while. I felt uncomfortable under her gaze; I didn't know what to expect.

She started talking. Her lips formed a tense, contrived smile and her eyes wandered. She asked whether I had liked the visitor. She was pretending it was sheer curiosity on her part. She asked what it was we had been talking about for so long. Then she said he liked me and that he thought I was very mature for my age. I did not know whether this was good or bad, but I smiled. Mother did not, usually, sit on my bed to engage in conversations or to pay me compliments. All of a sudden she put her hand on top of mine. Her hand was cold and I pulled mine out and hid it under the blanket. She stared at her empty hand as if wondering what it was doing there, then she sat very erect and lowering her eyes, asked very quietly, "Would you like . . . would you like a man like him . . . Would you like him for a father?"

I did not understand at first. What was it she meant? Why would I need to think about anything like this? Even if I did like Volodya, what connection would there be between liking him and wanting him for a father? I looked at her through narrowed eyes.

"What do you mean?

"Just this," she uttered with tears in her eyes. "Whether you would like him to become your father?"

I looked at her with disbelief. "What kind of a question is this? I have a father already! I like my father!" Then, looking straight into her eyes I uttered the word that had been hanging on my lips since yesterday. "You traitor!" I said through clenched teeth, "You traitor!" And I turned my face away from her and pressed it against the cool white wall.

THE RETURN

During the war, when I was a child, the one thing that I desired most was to have a doll of my own. I could remember the toys that I used to have before the war: the Shirley Temple doll, the enameled chicken that laid eggs, the cards with the Three Little Pigs that hung above my bed and the white stuffed doggie with black eyes. I also had a shiny red train with cellophane windows and comfortable upholstered seats. It was so different from the real trains in which we travelled inside Russia. They were dark and crowded and they smelled.

My toys appeared frequently in my dreams. They popped out of drawers and rolled on soft beds or were handed to me by smiling aunties in long dresses and round straw hats.

But usually I woke up in a cold room with no toys in it, and the dreams left only a memory that lingered with me throughout the day. When I recounted these dreams to my parents, they smiled sadly and said that when the war ended and we came back to Poland, I would have toys again. They told me that perhaps we would even find my nursery intact, for they had locked the door well before leaving.

I imagined that as soon as we arrived in Poland, I would walk into a room full of toys and bright furniture, where aunts and cousins wearing straw hats and silk dresses would calmly sip tea from porcelain cups. They would smile at me, the way they did in the family photographs, then offer me cakes and candy and hand me dolls in frilly outfits and stuffed animals with fluffy hair.

But when we did arrive in Poland, after a month-long journey in rust-red cattle cars, there were no pretty cousins with dolls waiting for us at the train station. Father's cousin Sol and his wife, Eva, were there. They had sallow faces and deeply set, sad eyes. They were dressed in gabardine coats and flannel hats with wide rims. Their smiles were kind but wistful, and they hugged Mother and Father sobbing, as if we had come for a funeral. They kissed me, too, and wet my face with their tears. They were speaking Yiddish, which I could not understand, and they kept repeating *"Yo, yo,"* and *"Azoy"* and nodding sadly in answer to my parents' anxious questions.

Cousin Sol picked me up then with one hand and with the other he grabbed one of our suitcases. He carried me to a buggy that was waiting at the corner, under a lantern that cast misty light on the street, climbed up and placed me on his knees. Mother, Father and cousin Eva climbed after us heavily. It started raining, and the driver, wearing an oilcloth cap and a cape, opened the accordion-like dark canopy above our heads.

"Narutovitcha Street, number 40," cousin Sol said, and the horse started a slow trot on the wet, shiny cobblestones of the dark street.

When we arrived there, we first crossed a large rectangular yard, and then climbed up narrow dimly-lit stairs. The landings were wet, for the window had no glass in them. Cousin Sol opened a door and brought us into a long corridor that smelled of mothballs and soapy water.

"To obtain a three room apartment in the town of Lodz these days is a real stroke of luck," Cousin Sol said. "The ghetto is in ruins and so are other parts of town." He sighed and took off his hat and his scarf, then led us to the end of the corridor. We entered a room which was illuminated by two small bulbs that dangled sadly beneath a magnificent crystal chandelier, which looked too large and too splendid there. The room was crowded with a strange assortment of things which did not fit together at all. A heavily carved mahogany credenza stood against one wall.

On top of it were piled books and dishes in great disarray. The old sofa was loaded with bedding—yellowish eiderdowns in dirty-gray damask covers and huge feather-filled pillows. Three open suitcases stood in the corner and just above them, on the windowsill, I saw jars filled with red preserves that gave out a sweet-sour smell of fermentation. I looked around carefully. Not a doll in sight. I tried to peep inside the large greenish wardrobe, the doors of which stood ajar. Only clothes spilled out of it in disarray.

"This is going to be our room," cousin Eva said. "You will live in the bedroom."

Mother smiled and sighed. Cousin Eva took her coat off and helped Mother out of hers. Then she led us to the kitchen. A cord was stretched diagonally across the bare room. Shirts, socks and underwear hung above huge steaming pots. Cousin Eva stirred the contents of a pot with a wooden ladle, then fished out a pair of steaming longjohns, which she dropped into a pail of cold water.

"You arrived on a laundry day," she said, and pinched my cheek with her wet hand. She had curly, black hair and a long nose on which sat heavy eyeglasses. She had a number written in blue on the inside of her arm and did not fit the image of a cousin that I had brought with me from Russia. But she was nice, and I could see that Father was fond of her, for he looked at her softly and often, took her hand and patted it sadly while she said, "All right, Leon dear, all right."

She took us to our room. It was cleaner and less crowded than the other room and was furnished with two large beds, a wardrobe with a clear, oval mirror and a small cot. A vase with fresh flowers stood on a night table next to the cot.

Mother looked at Cousin Eva gratefully. "Thank you. My God, what luxury!"

"After this war everything is a luxury!" answered cousin Eva, wiping her hands against her skirt. She then very gently took my coat off, folded it and put it on the bed. She sat down then, pulled me towards her, placed me between her knees and peered into my eyes, as if she was seeing there a reflection of someone she knew. She pressed me then quickly to her large, warm bosom, closed her eyes and patted my back gently. "Aaah," she moaned sadly, "Aaah."

Then she stood up, wiped her eyes with the back of her hand and pushed me gently towards the door. When we entered the living room the table was set for tea. Father was talking to cousin Sol in a hushed voice. I could see that his eyes were very sad. Mother, cousin Eva and I sat at the table. Cousin Eva poured the tea into glasses and handed one to me. I must have looked sad, for she leaned above me with concern. Her eyeglasses travelled to the tip of her nose.

"What's the matter? You don't like it here? You prefer it in Russia?" she said.

I was not certain that I liked it here or that I liked it more in Russia. I was not certain about anything at that moment. The only thing I knew was that all this was not the way I hoped it would be and not the way I had imagined. It was not all bad, and I liked cousin Eva and Sol even though they did not wear long dresses and straw hats. I also knew I did not want to offend them or make them even sadder than they were.

"Y . . . yes," I said, "I do like it here. But where are the dolls? I was promised dolls when I returned to Poland!"

Cousin Eva stared at me, taken aback, the tip of her chin pressed against her throat.

"Dolls? . . . Dolls . . . They were . . . They were . . . " she stuttered. Then she glanced at Mother and finished rather hurriedly. "They are in the stores, dear, there are many dolls in the toy-shops. You will take her to the toy-shops, Leon, won't you."

But Father was too busy talking to cousin Sol, and he did not answer.

At night, my mother told me that cousin Eva had a little daughter too, but she had been taken away from her.

"Like my dolls," I said.

"Yes, like your dolls."

I hoped that we would go to the toy stores the very next day. But we did not. On the days that followed, Father and I travelled by tramway and buggy to different parts of the city. Father knocked on doors and rang bells. Sometimes the doors remained closed, and sometimes a face appeared, staring at Father suspiciously. "No," they said, "we moved in here only recently. Never heard." Or they said, "Yes, yes, I remember. Disappeared one night, like so many." Father sometimes stopped to read lists that were posted on poles and went away saddened. "Nobody left," he sighed. "Who could have imagined? Nobody."

He seemed lost and his eyes wandered. His face was getting skinnier and darker. Sometimes he stumbled on the sidewalk and had to lean against a wall. I pulled on his hand and said, "Father, what's the matter, Father?" But he just stared at me sadly and did not answer, as if I too were not there.

Once we boarded a buggy and it kept going for a long time. After a while, I noticed that the houses we passed were smaller and stood at increasingly greater distances from each other. At one point, Father said, "Please stop here!" and the buggyman answered, "Nothing to stop here for, sir."

He was right; next to where we stopped, there was only a large pile of rubbish and fire-blackened bricks.

"Here stood our house," Father said. He got off the buggy and stood next to the pile of bricks with bowed head. His hat fell off, and a gust of wind carried it into a puddle. But he did not run after it. I climbed down from the buggy and stood next to him. He took my hand in his and clasped it till it hurt.

"Father," I said, "is that where my nursery was? The one you locked so well?"

He nodded. "Do you remember, really?" he said, astonished. "Yes."

"Your nursery too, my child."

I threw myself on the bricks. "Father, perhaps they are buried there . . . my dolls. Perhaps we can find them, perhaps we can still save them!" I cried. "Lift these bricks, Father!"

He did not react. I grabbed one of the bricks with both hands and moved it, then I moved a few more. All I saw underneath was more dark bricks. Father pulled me away.

"There is nothing here, you hear, nothing! Leave these bricks alone!" He was gasping and breathing heavily, and his eyes were bulging.

"There are no dolls under the bricks, you hear, nothing is left! Nothing!" He was almost screaming now, and I was scared. Then he let go of my hand and stared at the bricks with eyes in which there was no hope and almost no expression. It was as if this pile of bricks made him finally realize and believe something that he could not believe before. A dull pain and anger stole into my heart too. So that was it! It was all a lie! All their promises were just a simple lie and a deception. But I could not tell it to my father now, for he looked too sad with his tearing eyes, his hat rolling in the puddle behind him. So I just pulled on his hand again, and I hoped it hurt him. Then I started crying too. Then Father and I climbed together into the buggy, where the driver sat smoking a cigarette and staring at the empty, sad street.

On the second or third week after our arrival, Father finally took me to the main street of the city of Lodz. The street was called Ulitsa Pyotrkovska, and it looked as if bombs had never fallen on this part of the city at all. I looked around in wonder, for I had never seen such tall, massive buildings before, or such gleaming, large windows. There was a hotel on that street which was called Grand and which looked very grand indeed. Marble stairs led to a shiny, revolving door which was flanked by two palms in round pots. A movie house was next to the hotel. A man on a poster under the marquee looked as if he were trying to choke a blond-haired woman with large teeth, yet the woman was smiling. It all looked very strange and very wonderful and I stopped in the middle of the sidewalk. Father pulled me by the hand, saying that I could not stand there forever. We passed a flower shop and a book store with tall, bright windows; this too seemed magnificent and marvellous to me. Then we arrived at a coffee shop. I just stood in front of it as if I were nailed to the sidewalk, and no pulling or urging helped Father to budge me from there, for what I saw was a dream come true.

The window of that coffee shop was dark and sparkling, huge and marvellously clean, and it was decorated with letters and garlands of gold. Inside there stood round glass tables on curved metal legs. Elegantly dressed ladies in short, narrow skirts sat at the tables, ate cakes and drank tea from very thin glasses. They wore small hats decorated with stiff feathers and thin voiles which descended over their foreheads and eyes, which were large and accentuated with black pencil. Their lips were sharply outlined in dark red and their brows were even and shapely, as if they were painted on their faces. They held their long legs to the side of the chair and wore the thinnest stockings. Waitresses dressed in black served them from gleaming serving trays. This was more like the image of Poland that I brought with me than anything I had seen.

"This must be Poland now!" I said to Father, but he did not understand. "We have been in Poland for the last three weeks," he answered, adding that I behaved like a peasant on a first visit to a large city, and that people were beginning to stare at me. He pulled me away from the window of the coffee shop.

I had no time to reflect on what he said, for at that moment I saw what I had been looking forward to seeing from my first evening in Lodz. A sign above a shop across the street said, simply, "A Toy Shop" in bold, red and green letters. I pulled Father behind me. "Look, Father, look! Finally! A toy store!"

We crossed the street and I ran to the window and pressed my face against the glass. It had been a wonderful day, full of surprises, and this was a culmination of them all. "Look, Father, real dolls!" I cried, and looked up at him to see whether he shared any of my happiness. But he only smiled faintly and absentmindedly, as if his thoughts were on more important matters, though what could be more beautiful or more important I could not easily imagine. "Yes, real toy shop and real dolls," he repeated almost mechanically, and without any wonder in his voice. But his indifference did not affect me at all.

Already, I was in a world of my own. My eyes raced up and down as if I wanted to take in all the contents of this window at once. I was like a thirsty wanderer in a desert at an oasis. I was a princess coming to take possession of her long lost kingdom. I could not believe my eyes: all the toys from my dreams and my memories were assembled in that window. There seemed to be no end to these toys. They filled every space in the window, every shelf and every box. Red, blue and yellow parrots dangled inside wooden rings, and a red light flickered in a lantern. In the left corner stood three small chickens and above them hung cards with the Three Little Pigs. Stuffed dogs, cats, bear and mice made of cotton occupied the right side of the window. On the upper shelf were displayed books, and on the lower—cards sprinkled with golden dust. Most magnificent, however, were the dolls, which occupied the center of the display: large dolls in beautiful dresses, and middle-sized dolls in school uniforms, baby dolls that were sucking on pacifiers and very tiny dolls for doll houses. I had never imagined that there were so many toys in the whole world. I would have remained standing there forever, but Father was pulling on my hand again. He was saying something about a person he had made a business appointment with and that we had to hurry along. I resisted and begged to stay a little longer, but Father insisted; he said the appointment was important for him. I relented finally, and trotted behind him reluctantly, all the while turning back to catch another glimpse of the wonderland that so suddenly and miraculously appeared before me.

When, a few weeks later, I was allowed to go out on my own, I headed for the toy store right away. I was afraid lest something had happened to the store in the meantime. So many people and things had disappeared in this place, that a toy store could disappear too. So I ran instead of walked, and I arrived out of breath. To my relief, the store was still there and as full of wonders as it had been when I had first seen it. I examined each one of the dolls slowly and carefully, and noticed every detail. Some of the dolls wore panties and socks; I never had any socks and only one pair of panties. I tried to decide which of the toys I wanted most. This was not something I could make a quick decision about; I wanted them all.

After I had been standing in front of the window for a while, I decided to go in. I gasped as I entered, for the inside of the store was even more wonderful than the window. It was a Sesame and I was Ali Baba. There was only one saleslady in the store and no other customers. The saleslady looked like a doll herself. She was dressed in a dainty, frilly, white blouse, had blond curly hair, blue eyes and the reddest painted lips. She wore shoes on thick high heels and moved slowly and carefully, as if operated by a spring mechanism that was slowing down.

The saleslady eyed me curiously up and down. I blushed, for I was dressed in a coat which had been given to me by the Committee for War Refugees. The coat was too large and made me look and feel awkward. My hair looked awkward too, for it was cut short, like a boy's. The girls here wore long braids with ribbons or ringlets that fell softly to their shoulders.

Something in the pleading expression of my eyes must have touched the saleslady, for she smiled kindly.

"What is it that you want, little girl?" she asked.

"How much is the tiniest doll in the window?" I said, very fast. "The one in the green frock?"

"This one? It's only thirty zloty."

I gasped again. What did she mean by 'only'? Thirty zloty was a lot of money. A few days before, Father, Mother and I had stopped in front of a confectionery, which displayed in its window marvels made of sugar, cream and cake, the likes of which I had not seen or tasted even in my dreams. Mother licked her lips, and asked Father whether we had enough for a cake. He stared at her with great astonishment and asked whether she had gone out of her mind. Mother was ashamed and turned away from that window sadly. That cake was thirty zloty too.

I breathed in and, gathering all my courage, told the saleslady that this was more than I had with me. "I shall return when I get my allowance," I said.

I felt very important for a minute when I said the world allowance. I read the word in a book which I had found in the apartment. Cousin Eva explained the meaning of the word to me, but I suspected it was only in stories that children received allowances. Whenever I mentioned money to my parents, they looked at me very sternly and reproachfully and said I should not forget they were only poor immigrants who had nothing but the skin on their bodies. They reminded me that I should be grateful for the bread and the white soft rolls we could now have every day and without rationing cards, and for the meat we could some-times buy. I tried my best to be grateful, but I knew I wanted a small doll more than I wanted the rolls and the meat, and that I would sacrifice them readily if given the chance.

But no one seemed willing to give me that chance or to buy a doll for me. Everyone seemed to have important matters and concerns on his mind, and the little money there was, was always urgently needed. Cousin Eva and Sol had no time for me. They were preparing to leave. Everybody seemed to be in constant, feverish motion: running, meeting, talking, unpacking, crying, laughing, hugging. So every day I wandered to Ulitsa Pyotrkovska and stood in front of the toy shop for a long time, my nose pressed against the thick, cool glass.

The world stopped existing for me then. I was only dimly

aware of the stream of people moving behind me, laughing, talking, tapping with their heels, or of the passing traffic and of the other children who sometimes briefly stopped next to me, then went on their way. I gave names to the dolls in the window: Lalla, and Katya and Marysia. I enjoyed locating them each day and greeted them as if they were old friends.

One day, Lalla, my favorite doll, and the one I wanted most of all, had disappeared, and in her place was a strange new doll with a vacant expression and heavy legs made of flesh-coloured material. A sign placed next to it said the doll was one of the first products of a new toy factory operated by the Union of Communist Workers. I was very upset and I entered the store hoping to find her there. The saleslady said she had just sold Lalla the other day. I wanted to know whether the girl who received the doll was pretty and rich, whether she had braids with ribbons and whether she was happy to get it. The saleslady looked at me with a bemused expression and said she did not know, for the doll was bought by an older gentleman who looked like a grandfather.

I went out saddened and tried to imagine that girl and I wished I had a grandfather too. I was sure that girl did not need to wear clothes from the Committee for War Refugees. I was also sure she had good parents who never complained about money and a father with a job. I returned to our apartment house and went to play in the yard. At least here I was like other children, for out in the yard most of the children had no toys. My new friend, Halina, did have a doll, but it was old and dirty and wore patched dresses. I envied Halina even this old and dirty doll, for when we played with her we forgot she was old. She could be a princess or a gently nanny, or a baby: she could be whatever we wanted. I asked Halina whether we could name her doll Lalla, and she agreed it would be her middle name, which was very consoling to me.

Cousins Eva and Sol left Poland and we took possession of the room with the chandelier. We were assigned a couple of tenants, a Mrs. Sarah Lubochinska and her daughter Sabena, who moved into the third, small room.

One summer day something quite wonderful and unexpected happened. My mother's friend Marysia came for a visit from the town of Plotsk, where she lived. She arrived carrying a valise and a large square box wrapped in newspaper and tied with a string. Aunt Marysia was a colourful, happy person and I had loved her since her first visit with us, in the spring. She entered the apartment bringing with her the smell of pleasant perfume and the sound of her vibrant laughing voice and of her heels rapping against the floor. She marched into the living room as if she was about to take possession of it, and placed the box on the table. I hopped behind her, happy to see her again.

"It's for you!" she said, pointing to the box. She sat on the sofa, smiling, panting and sweating and fanning herself with a paper fan. Her eyes had frivolous sparks in them, and I suspected that she was pulling my leg.

"For me? Really? What is it, auntie Marysia?"

"Open it and you'll see."

I hoped it was a doll. Shaking with excitement, I ran to the kitchen to fetch a knife. I returned very fast and cut the string loose. Then I took the newspaper off. There was a cardboard box inside. Marysia helped me open it. I peeped into the box and saw something that looked like a small red roof. Aunt Marysia put her hands in and pulled the roof up. I looked up and saw that it was a doll house she was holding in her arms. I stared at her astonished and unbelieving, hardly daring to breathe.

"A real doll house? Is it really for me, aunt Marysia?"

She laughed loudly. "Of course, you small idiot, who else in this house could it be for?"

I approached the doll house with awe and touched it with the tip of my finger, as if I was afraid it would disintegrate if I touched it with my whole hand. The doll house was made of thin metal that felt cool and smooth when touched. I stepped back and smiled happily. It was a perfect doll house, neither too big nor too small. It had a living room, a dining room and a kitchen on the first floor, and two bedrooms on the second. It was white on the outside and had four windows with shutters. Flower boxes were painted beneath the windows. It also had a fence that folded and unfolded and a few sunflowers were painted on the side wall.

"Such happiness, auntie Marysia!" I exclaimed. "You cannot imagine how happy I am!"

When Father returned from town, he kissed aunt Marysia, obviously pleased to see her. Then he saw the doll house and turned it around appreciatively. "Some doll house you've got here," he said. "A real pre-war doll house, I would say." I pranced and danced around the table, then around the two of them. Aunt Marysia looked at me pensively, then said to Father quietly, "I guess she did not have a childhood at all."

"No, not at all," Father answered and patted me on the head.

I stared at the doll house for a while longer, then I examined the details. I peeped into the rooms and tested the shutters. The shutters worked and the fence looked lovely around the imaginary garden. The rooms were empty, but they were wall papered. Round carpets were painted on the floors. I threw myself on aunt Marysia's neck.

"Thank you so very much. From now on and forever, you are my favorite person."

Father helped me to transfer the doll-house to the bedroom and placed it on my night table, next to my cot. I stared at it, happy, till I fell asleep.

Aunt Marysia went away, and I remained with the empty doll house. I often sat staring at it, trying to imagine how it was going to look furnished, and inhabited by a family of dolls. I planned to sew the curtains, the blankets and the pillows from scraps of materials I was going to get from the seamstress, Mrs. Novitzka. But I needed the furniture and the dolls before I could do that.

The doll house remained standing on my night table, and I could see it as soon as I woke up. I placed it there in a way that allowed the rays of sun to come in through the small windows, the square frames of which lay their checkered imprints on the floors. When I went to the toy shop, it was with a definite purpose: to choose the furniture and the dolls for my doll house. After a few visits, I had a detailed plan and everything, down to the kitchen cupboard, chosen and arranged.

In the fall, I started going to school. I was looking forward to it; for I remembered the stories from Father and Mother's school days that I had heard in Russia. These stories were full of pleasant memories of fun and mischief, eccentric but kind teachers and bright classmates. I thought I would enter into the world of these memories as soon as I crossed the wrought iron gate of the school and mounted the stairs, where a severe janitor with a large moustache was standing ringing the shiny brass bell.

But things turned out not to be as simple and as attractive as I thought. Most schools taught religion; Mother and Father had decided I was not going to learn things I did not believe and I agreed with them. I could not go to a Jewish school, for I did not speak Yiddish. The only alternative was The Democratic Worker's School, but enrollment there was limited.

"You must understand, Madame," Mrs. Urbanska, the principal, said to Mother. "Our ratio of Jews is too high. We are already considered a Jewish school."

"But I thought that in the new communist regime all were equal, and it did not matter, Jew or non-Jew," Mother said.

The principal, who wore a gray tunic and sported a short mannish haircut, started rearranging some papers on her desk. "This is all I can tell you, madame," she said without raising her eyes.

An atmosphere of nervous mourning descended upon our home. Mother threw me despondent looks, and I sometimes felt things would have been better for all concerned had I not been born. The future loomed bleak and hopeless. I was a person who just did not fit anywhere. There were other children, for whom things seemed to proceed with ease, but I was not one of them.

My salvation came unexpectedly. One day, Father came home beaming. He had just found out that Yezhy Yurchik, who used to be a worker in my grandfather's factory before the war, was now a high official in the Ministry of Education. Father had obtained an interview with him. Mother was overjoyed. She patted me on the head and went to break the news to Mrs. Lubochinska and to Sabena, who took an active interest in my future. I was to accompany Father to Mr. Yurchik's office. After all, he knew me as a baby and this could help my prospects.

Father and I went to see Mr. Yurchik a few days later. His office was located in the nicest building on Ulitsa Pyotrkovska, not far from the toy shop. We went to the top floor by elevator and were admitted into a sunny room which was furnished with expensive looking antiques. Above a heavily sculpted and gold-bordered commode, hung a portrait of Stalin. A portrait of Lenin decorated the opposite wall. The president of Poland, Mr. Byerut, was there too, but in a smaller frame. They all seemed to be smiling victoriously. The man who greeted us had a victorious smile on his face too. He leaned across the desk to clasp my father's hand, then sank into a leather chair, clasping his hands in front of him. He was a skinny man with blond hair and blond complexion, and both the room and the chair seemed too large for him. He smiled in a peculiar way and said, "So, Leon, who would have ever thought, ah?"

Father smiled back, not at all joyfully, I thought. He glanced appreciatively around and his eyes rested on the gold borders of the frames and the furniture. He congratulated Mr. Yurchik on his postion. They exchanged some memories and mentioned some names, then Father told him, stuttering slightly, what he had come for.

Comrade Yurchik was very obliging.

"But of course, what wouldn't I do for a son of my former employer . . . " he said. "He was like a father to me, capitalist or not."

Then he rang his secretary, who produced a letter for us. We parted from Yezhy Yurchik and went down the street. I tried to pull my father to the toy shop; but he scolded me, saying something about the seriousness of the matter we had attended to and its importance for my future and that I should stop being such a child.

With the letter in hand, Mother led me back to Mrs. Urbanska's office. On the way there she muttered, "Who would have thought we would have to face this. We might as well have remained in Russia." All flushed, she knocked on the principal's door. She handed the letter to her and the principal read it attentively.

"My God, a letter from Comrade Yurchik himself!" she said respectfully. "We'll make a place for her, even if we don't have any."

That evening we celebrated with a chicken dinner. After dinner we invited Mrs. Lubochinska and Sabena for tea. We clinked glasses and all drank to my future.

The next day I went to school, but it was not the same as in my parents' stories. The children looked at me as if I were an animal of an unknown species, and they laughed at my shorn hair and at my clothes. The teacher seemed neither eccentric nor kind. She had tightly pursed lips and wore her hair in a bun that jutted up above her heavy neck, which was covered with bristly gray hairs. She asked me whether I knew the irregular verbs. I did not even know what verbs were, and she gave me a long list to memorize for the next day. The girl who sat next to me asked what my surname was and then said I must be Jewish, a *"zhydovka."* She said it scornfully and I looked at her hurt and surprised. In Russia nobody seemed interested in surnames and the kind Uzbecks of Samarkand were not interested in my nationality at all. We were just refugees and non-refugees there. But Poland was my motherland and I thought I was not a refugee and a stranger anymore.

I came home sad and disappointed. I sat and stared at my doll house, but its empty interiors offered no consolation. The yard was empty, the other kids were at school. I knew suddenly that I must do something about this doll house, that it just could not stand there useless and empty, but nothing came to my mind. So I curled up in my bed and cried.

About the time I started going to school, my father started his new job in the Government Institute of Salvage and Recycling. He bought an elegant, dark suit and a tie for himself. In the mornings, he shaved carefully and sprinkled cologne all over his face and neck, so that he smelled nice. Mother laughed at him a little and said he smelled like a small flower garden. She also asked whether there were any pretty ladies working at his office. But I thought this was so much nicer than when he was a truck driver in Russia and smelled of gasoline and alcohol. I liked the way he looked now. When he bought a new briefcase with brass initials, he looked awfully impressive. Even the janitor noticed and addressed him as "Sir Director." The briefcase was made of real leather and smelled pleasant too. One day, Father came home smiling broadly and announced that the janitor was right, for he had been nominated director of his department. When he looked at himself in the oval mirror that evening, he thrust his chest forward a little and lifted his shoulders.

About a week after his announcement, my parents entertained guests for the first time. They bought vodka, sweet liqueurs and cold cuts. Mother bought a new dress for the occasion, and black shoes with metal buckles and high heels. She had her eyebrows plucked thin and her eyelashes dyed with henna and she looked like an aged actress in a silent film. Father put on his new suit and a tie with thin silver stripes. Seeing all these purchases, I gathered all my courage and asked Mother whether I could, perhaps, get some furniture for the doll house. But Mother said that what they were buying was not a luxury, that it was a necessity, that if one wanted to get ahead anywhere in this world, one needed to "look good" and to maintain "good relations with people." She said that furniture for a doll house was something only rich people could afford.

The guests brought cakes in white cardboard boxes tied with shiny thin ribbons. I knew those cakes. They were the ones that cost thirty zloty each, and I stared at them with awe and respect. Each could buy a small doll. I was served a mushroom that had a leg of meringue, white cream inside the leg, and a red head dotted with tiny cream spots. That mushroom tasted of heaven. To eat it all at once seemed like a sin and a sacrilege; I wrapped the cream-filled leg in a napkin and hid it in the kitchen of my doll house.

When Father was installed in his new office, he invited me to come in to see it. The office was bright and large and resembled the office of comrade Yurchik. Stalin, Lenin and President Byerut were hanging here too. The portraits were smaller, though, and not as smiling, as if the Institute of Salvage and Recycling was not a place to smile that radiantly. The frames were not bordered with gold, but the room had an enclosed balcony of its own and thin, white curtains hung in the wide windows. Pots of red geraniums stood on the windowsill. A secretary came in and watered them carefully from a brass can. Father sat at a massive desk of dark wood. His armchair was deep and looked comfortable, and his name was engraved on a brass plate in cursive, calligraphed letters.

After I touched all the knobs and buttons on his desk and lifted a telephone receiver to check whether the phone was real, I sat in a chair across from Father and stared at him. Was it really my father sitting there, so good looking and so important and so different from the way he had looked just about a year ago, in Russia? So finally my father had a nice office and work that he seemed to like. For as long as I could remember him, he had done things that I knew he did not want to do and did not like.

As soon as we arrived in Russia, he was mobilized into the army. He did not want to go to the army, and he tried to convince the officer who came to our house that he wouldn't do any good there, that he was an artist, that he was not material for the army at all. But he was taken away and sent us pictures of himself in a uniform and a hat with flaps that looked like ass's ears.

When he was released, he started working as a truck driver for a bakery, and he did not like that either. He came home after his first day on the job as if he were the baker himself, for he was white to the eyeballs and when he sat down clouds of flour came from him, and we all spat and sneezed. He did not like that job because the drivers at the bakery stole and pressed him to steal too, which he did not want to do. Then all the drivers got fired from that bakery for suspected theft, and Father was fired too. Mother said to him then, "You see the reward that you got for your honesty. Next time you won't be so honest."

He did not disappoint her, for his next "work" was in smuggling contraband, and he really hated that. But he had to do it, for he could find no other job. "Red Yankl," the driver, came with an offer and talked about it enticingly. Father refused adamantly at first, but then Mother said to him, "You'll be stubborn, and we shall die of hunger," and that convinced him to take the job.

Red Yankl introduced Father to "Ahmad the Blind" who knew the mountains the way one knows the palm of one's hand, and the three of them drove an old battered truck in which they travelled through mountainous, wild terrain. Father's face was tense and unhappy at that time. He often came home drunk. I heard him stumbling on the stairs and asking, "Does Leon live here?" which might have sounded funny, except that it was not. He wore stained overalls, and when he tried to kiss me, he smelled of alcohol, gasoline and tobacco.

Father looked at me from across the desk, smiling.

"What's this wandering look in your eyes? Where have your thoughts travelled?" he asked.

"Back to Samarkand," I said. "I remembered the jobs that you held there, and the cabin of the old battered truck."

Father laughed loudly. "And the way I came home from the bakery all white . . . "

"This too."

"What a difference!"

"Yeah!"

Father asked me to come over to him. He placed me on his knees and patted my head softly. Then he rang a bell, and his secretary came in, her heels clicking on the tile floor. He asked for some tea and cookies, and she brought them in after a while. I returned to my seat and drank my tea seriously, the way adults do, taking in quiet sips and without slurping. Father sat across from me, drank his tea too, and we smiled at each other.

My mother began working too, and I frequently remained home all alone. I still wandered to the store, though not as frequently as before. More and more of the old dolls disappeared from the display, and the new ones were all made by the new factory and were not the kind of dolls that I would want to have. One wore a red kerchief on her neck, another wore overalls and held a hammer. As the old dolls left, I felt sad. It was like parting from old friends. This also meant that there were more and more girls receiving dolls, and that I was not one of them.

And so, my doll house remained empty. I was a little better dressed now, for Mother had some of the clothing that we had received from the committee converted to fit me. But whenever she paid the dressmaker, she made such a fuss about it that I never dared to ask her for even the tiniest doll. When I did mention a doll once, she told me I was a big blunderbuss and should be eyeing boys instead of desiring little dolls and furnishings for a doll house. I was hurt and astonished. I could not see how she could make this kind of comparison; the boys in my class had pimples and freckles and were not much to look at. "Disgusting is what they are!" I told her and decided not to bring up the subject of dolls with her anymore.

While my doll house stood bare and neglected, things were getting lively in our home. We had a telephone installed, which was a rare privilege. Mother had new acquaintances who wore elegant clothes and to whom she talked very sweetly, using many diminutive words like "darling," "loved heart" and "treasure." Father talked office and business, walking back and forth around the telephone, repeating and stressing many words. Mother bought sardines, vodka and dry sausage to serve to guests, who were frequently dropping by in the evenings.

It was on the occasion of one of those visits that I found my first fifty zloty banknote. While Mother and Father entertained a dinner guest in the living room, I went to the bedroom to search the closet for a dress to wear to school next day. When I opened the door of the closet, a shaft of light fell on its floor and I saw, lying there, a red fifty zloty note. The face of an old gentleman stared at me from that banknote; he was smiling at me kindly and curiously, as if he were challenging and warning me at the same time. I stared back at him greedily and with surprise. The banknote must have fallen from Mother's or Father's coat pocket.

I crouched and reached out my hand to take the bill, but I drew it back right away. What if . . . I hesitated. At first I wanted to leave it there and forget about it. That gentleman had sharp eyes, which could be kind, but which held some strange power, and I felt that the power was not all benign. I was tempted, and yet afraid. But then, I turned to face the room and I saw my empty doll house. I knew that in that closet lay two little dolls in the shape of a square piece of paper. It was an opportunity that might not repeat itself that soon. I made my decision fast. Facing the closet I crouched again, took the bill into my hand, crumpled it, threw it to the dark corner at the rear of the closet and pushed it even deeper with the tip of my shoe. Then I closed the closet door as quickly and as quietly as I could and, with my heart pounding, sat on the bed. I touched my cheeks: they were hot. My hands were sweating. I was strangely excited; afraid and yet happy.

I decided to risk nothing and leave the money there for a while, till all the danger was over, till I could be sure. Then I went to my desk to do my homework. The lamp on the desk seemed to give a warmer than usual glow, and the doll house seemed to smile at me contentedly.

I regarded my parents tensely the next morning. They went to work as usual. In the evening, I waited shakily for their return. I thought they would notice the loss instantly, though I hoped they wouldn't. Fifty zloty appeared to be such a large sum of money; when the dressmaker had asked Mother fifty zloty for an alteration of a dress for me, Mother came out with such an outcry that I was sure the dressmaker was robbing her of her last penny. She finally brought the price down to forty zloty and came out looking victorious. The dressmaker sighed when she took the money, and I felt sorry for her: she lived in one small room and looked poor.

To my surprise and secret joy, neither Mother nor Father mentioned any loss. Their lives went on as usual, completely unaffected by the absence of the fifty zloty bill. When the end of that week came, I knew that the banknote was mine.

So, on a Saturday morning, as soon as Mother and Father left, I opened the closet and peeked into the corner. The bill was there and as red as the Russian flag. I grabbed it fast, and, lifting my skirt, tucked it into my underwear. From there, I transferred it to my pillow for two more days. It rustled pleasantly and dangerously when I touched the corner of the pillow case where it was hidden. Soon it was going to be converted into one or two little dolls.

On Monday afternoon, as soon as my parents left, I went to the pillow and took the bill out, stealthily put it in my coat pocket and sneaked out of the house. In the street, I walked close to the walls. It seemed to me that what I had just done was written all over me. My face kept getting hot, cold, then hot again. I hoped I would not meet anyone I knew. It took ages to get to the toy shop.

As soon as I walked into the shop, however, all my fears and apprehensions vanished as if touched by a magic spell. Everything was quiet, orderly and colourful here, and the saleslady wore her pleasant smile and her frilly white blouse. When she leaned above me, her generous bosom hovered just above my head protectively. All of a sudden I felt safe, important, pretty, wise and rich. I was, finally, a customer, not only a pitiable looker into windows. The dolls stared enticingly at me from the shelves as if asking to be bought and I smiled back at them.

"So, little girl, have you received your allowance yet?" she asked. She remembered me! I felt happier and even more important.

"Yes, I did!" I said, and I pulled the fifty zloty bill from my pocket, looking at it expectantly. With a touch of disappointment I remarked that she was not too impressed with my red bill. It might not be such a big sum after all. As if to reconfirm my suspicion, she said that I could not have very much for that money. I said that I did not want very much, that all I wanted was the tiny doll in the green frock, who sat at the edge of the window. I grabbed the saleslady's hand and pulled her out of the store to point the doll to her. "I have a doll house, you see!" I said loudly, so that the girl who stood next to me just then could hear. The girl did glimpse at me enviously, and the saleslady said with mock seriousness, "Oh, so you have a doll house too. How very wonderful!" Then she reentered the store, took a long pole, fished the doll from the window, took it off the metal hook and handed it to me.

I took the tiny doll with my two fingers and put her gently in the palm of my other hand. She was truly delightful. Although she was very small, her eyes opened and closed, and she had a sweet face, and arms and legs that moved. The saleslady suggested that for the twenty zloty left I should buy a small wooden bed, and I agreed by nodding to her, not daring to let my eyes off the sweet doll.

"I shall name her Malla, the little one, for she is so small," I told the saleslady when she handed the bed to me, and she acknowledged the information with a solemn nod. When I lifted my face to look at her again, I saw that she was staring at me thoughtfully. Her mouth curved down as if she was going to cry. I thought it was because she too did not like to be parting with her dolls.

I left the store a happy person. I carried the bed with Malla in it in my arms all the way home, and so many people in the street smiled and chatted with me that my happiness was complete. It was a sunny, warm day, and the leaves that fell off the chestnut trees that lined Narutovitcha street gave it a pleasant glow. They rustled under my feet as I walked, and it was as if I were treading upon a rich, orange-red carpet. I looked up: the trees were making friendly noises at me when the wind moved their branches. The windows of the tall houses glistened gaily, like many bright eyes, and the giant gray figures that carried a balcony on their backs seemed to be looking at me from above with a glee. The world approved of my purchase.

When I came home, I placed the bed in the little bedroom and stood watching it. Then I folded a handkerchief in four and covered the little doll. I could see how lovely the doll house would be all furnished and with a family of dolls living there. I was now one step closer to the realization of my dream. I knew I did not want Malla to be an only child, like me. I wanted Malla to have a sister she could play with, a Mother who would take care of her and a Father who would read books to her and help her with the homework.

Before I went to sleep, I turned the doll house towards me, so that I could see Malla in her bedroom. The memory of the way I obtained the fifty zloty was gnawing inside me, but my happiness made me disregard and forget it. I was also pleased with the way my parents took my announcement that the doll was a present from a school friend. Father went on reading his newspaper, and Mother just nodded. I could sleep peacefully.

But Malla's presence in the doll house made the other rooms appear even emptier by comparison. I searched the closet floor diligently, but no one seemed inclined to lose any more bills for my sake. Then, one day, as I was staring dreamily into the warm, dark interior of the closet in which hung my parent's coats and suits, without even thinking I put my hand into Mother's pocket. Quite a few bills rustled in that pocket and I closed my fist on one and pulled it out. Just then I heard Mother's steps, and I repeated my manouever: I crumpled the bill into a ball and threw it into the dark corner of the closet. I was shaking when she entered the room, but the room was dim and she did not notice my confusion. When she had gone, I crawled into the closet and saw that this time it was a brown 100 zloty bill, and the gentleman whose portrait stared from it appeared quite preoccupied with other than my theft matters, for his eyes stared boldly and confidently ahead.

But I was not as bold and confident as he was, and the days that followed were not very serene for me. In the morning I ran to school thinking about the 100 zloty bill. During the classes my mind wandered to the closet in fear, worry and anticipation. My mother's stern and unforgiving face haunted me constantly. The teacher caught me inattentive and placed me in the corner. When I came home I scanned Mother's face, searching for signs of suspicion, anger or sorrow. I eavesdropped on her conversations with Father. I lived in a state of great tension for more than two weeks.

One day, when the coast was clear, I dared to peep into the closet. Then, very cautiously, I crawled in and rolled the crumpled paper ball out of the corner. I smoothed it out on the closet floor and placed it in the pocket of my coat. Then I put the coat on, slipped out of the room and ran straight to the toy-shop. "I've got it!" I waved the 100 zloty bill at the saleslady. "An uncle from Warshaw came for a visit and give it to me!"

"Wonders never cease!" she said and appeared almost as pleased as I was. She lay before me, on the wide counter, a large selection of small dolls and furniture. I stared at them the way a thief stares at his loot, carefully and greedily. After much deliberation, I chose a few pieces of furniture for the living room and one small doll. The saleslady wrapped my purchases in pretty paper decorated with smiling children's faces and tied the parcel with a thin pink ribbon. It was the end of her last spool, she said, a remnant from "the good old days."

My parents were not at home when I came back with the parcel. I turned the doll house around so that one could not see the interiors. I named the second doll Meela—the pleasant one.

It was fall then, and it rained frequently. The mornings were gray and grim, promising nothing but rain. The afternoons were gray, grim and wet. The tall dark chimneys of the many textile factories of Lodz poured out clouds of smoke and soot and laid dirty haze on the city. Our apartment smelled of humidity, soap and food. Only my doll house was beautiful, bright and clean. I sewed curtains and blankets from scraps of cotton, and rugs from pieces of thin felt. The dolls sat in the living room and read books I had made for them. Hans Christian Andersen's stories reaffirmed my belief that toys had lives and souls of their own and could experience happiness, sorrow and pain.

I became much happier then myself. My marks at school were better, and I liked the way I looked, for my hair grew, and I could put a barrette above my ear. I did not plan any more expeditions into my mother's pockets. But just then, quite unexpectedly, an opportunity presented itself and a temptation I was not strong enough to resist. It was when one evening I came into the living room and saw Father counting money which was piled before him on the table. He divided the banknotes into smaller bundles, which he then tied with elastics. I sat across from him and watched him count the money with great interest. The bills were large, red and green, and I saw *500* and *1000* written on them. There were thousands of zloty on that table.

Suddenly, the telephone rang in the hallway, and Father went to answer it. I got up very quickly and snatched a bill from the largest pile. Then I pushed it under the carpet just as quickly. I ran to the chair and sat down stiff and shivering and tense. I was amazed at myself; I was becoming a professional thief—and I knew what their end was.

Father came back and returned to his counting. I was shaking inside. The size of the bill and the magnitude of my crime frightened me. I did not like that feeling, and I wished I had not taken the bill. But it could not be undone. Taking money from Father was somehow different from taking it from Mother, for my father had weary, sad eyes that seemed to hide some great sorrows, and I frequently felt sorry for him. At my age he was already an orphan. But then, I thought, Father had all this money to count, and he never gave me any. He never gave me any presents. He should have known how much I wanted the dolls and the furniture. He should have bought them for me. These thoughts made the burden of my offence easier to bear and to think about. I became calm enough to stand up and march to the bedroom, where my doll house was standing waiting for me. Outside, the full moon looked like a large coin.

There remained the matter of hiding and disposing of the money. It was a 500 zloty bill and I had never held a bill that big in my hands. The gentleman that stared from it had a long beard and fierce, piercing eyes, and I did not like him staring at me for too long. I hid the bill in the pillow again. Its stuffed corner looked like a stiff little horn. I covered the pillow with my blanket. I needed a new plan, and a few days after I came up with one.

According to the plan, I was to march into the corner grocery store, where we did not usually shop, and buy some provisions there, which I did. I bought bread and sausage and received 350 zloty change. Then I went out to the street, where I was to dispose of the bread. I found a waste basket attached to a pole of a lantern, and looking left and right threw the bread in. The bread landed on a bunch of newpapers. But something was not right about throwing the bread away. It was a shapely loaf of rye bread, and it smelled fresh and delicious. I suddenly remembered how hungrily I ate the small slices of rationed black bread in Russia. A memory of the bakery where Father worked returned too. He had smelled like this bread when he came after work. I fished the bread out of the waste basket and put it back into the shopping net. Then I went to the small park next to St. Boniface's church. I sat on the bench, broke a piece off the loaf, and ate it with the sausage. A few pigeons were walking serenely and proudly on the gravel path as if it belonged to them. I crumbled some bread for them. One of them had a red eye that seemed to be observing me suspiciously. I threw him a larger crumb and went home. Whatever remained of the bread went to the pantry; I knew Mother was absent-minded enough not to notice.

A few weeks later, my doll house was almost completely furnished; I had a family of mother, father and two daughters living in it comfortably. I had to order the Father doll, for they had none in the store. He had a girl doll's face, but was wearing a black suit and a tie. It looked very funny. But the whole family together looked just magnificent when seated around the dining room table. I formed food out of plasticine and bread paste, used thimbles as cups and cut plates out of stiff white cardboard.

One day Father stopped next to me as I was playing with the dolls. I was apprehensive and scared for a moment. What if he looks too closely and becomes suspicious...? I looked at him from the corner of my eye. He stood there with a look of surprise on his face, as if he was seeing the doll house for the first time. Then he said, softly, "Let's see what you have got there," and he crouched next to me. His face was next to mine as he peered curiously inside. I gave him a short tour of the doll house and introduced the dolls to him. He too found the Father doll very droll and we laughed together. Then he said, "You have got there a nicer house than ours." I nodded, a little proudly and a little sadly. Then Father said, suddenly and unexpectedly, that what he thought this little house really needed now was electricity.

"Electricity?!" I exclaimed. I had never even considered such a thing feasible. "Who could install electricity in my doll house?!"

"I shall install it for you," Father said, as if it were a small matter for him, indeed, and he promised to buy the tools and the materials.

I was very happy. My own Father was going to install electricity for me! Life did have some pleasant surprises for me too! I thought guiltily about the 500 zloty, but there was nothing I could do about it now.

Father came home from work one evening and brought the thin wires, the tiny bulbs, the screwdrivers and the wire cutters. Soon after supper, he started working on the doll house. He sat on the floor cross-legged and looked like a little boy. He smiled to himself as if he was trying to figure out the best way to install the electrical system. I looked at him and hardly recognized him. We both sat on the floor, with the doll house between us, and I handed him the tools and the wires he needed.

It was very quiet. Mother was away at a Union of Newspaper Employees' meeting, and there were no noises coming from the yard. The radio was playing quietly in the other room and Father said, "Now the clippers and now the drill and now the small nails." I asked him whether he had ever done electric installation in a doll house, and he answered that he had once tried, for a small girl he was in love with, but that he had messed up her doll house instead and lost all his chances. He smiled cockily at the memory. It was the first time Father had told me anything about himself as a boy and I was happy and curious and I wanted to know more about him and the little girl he was talking about. I tried to imagine how a girl he was in love with looked, and I asked him whether she looked a little like me and he said yes, that she did, but I was much prettier. I laughed and rolled on the floor merrily. Then I began worrying lest he would mess up my doll house too, but he said he had grown up since and gained much experience with his trucks. Nevertheless, I was not totally convinced he could really do it, that it was at all possible.

At the end of the evening the tiny bulbs were installed in all the rooms and Father said, "Let's see now!" and inserted the plug into the electrical outlet. The little rooms were lighted as if by magic.

I turned off the electricity in the bedroom, and the doll house shone and sparkled in the dark. The doll family sat around the dining table, well-dressed and smiling, the rooms were neat and well-furnished and upstairs cozy bedrooms with blankets and curtains that I had sewn waited for them. It was a wonderful moment. I looked up at Father. He too was smiling, stooping slightly above the doll house. The lights illuminated his face, and his eyes shone in the dark. He had a handsome profile. "You see, this time I did not mess it up!" he said proudly. I put my hand in his, and we both stood there silently for a long while.

Because of the doll house, I became a very popular person. All my friends from school wanted to see it and made pilgrimages to my house after classes. They were obviously envious, which gave me a feeling of importance. They stayed for hours to play. We arranged weddings, birthday parties and outings to the balcony. We read books to them. We told them about a school they were going to attend when they were grown up. After a while the children from the yard started coming too, and I was never lonely.

Emboldened by my success, I continued my hunt for money. All of sudden, there was plenty of money rolling around. Once, Father left his wallet in the bathroom, and I found it lying on the small shelf. Mother frequently left change on the kitchen table and forgot all about it. I began forgetting to return the change from the grocer and no one remembered to ask for it. I was now receiving a small allowance from my parents, but it was only enough for candy. I urgently needed more things for the dolls. Malla needed a carriage, Father doll could use a small car; my own father was about to get one from the office. Money was slowly accumulating in the pillow case.

One evening I decided to withdraw some money from my "account." The saleslady had told me that the very nice carriage that she had in the store was the last one in stock. It cost 200 zloty and was a major investment. But I imagined Malla in the carriage and no sum of money seemed too large an investment.

On that evening I brushed my teeth, put my nightie on, said "Goodnight" to my parents in my sweetest and most innocent voice, and left them listening to the radio in the living room. Then I entered the bedroom, closed the door tightly and sat on my bed. I pulled the pillow out, unfastened the pillow case and emptied its contents on the mattress. Then I stretched the blanket over my head. I felt like one of the forty thieves entering Sesame and eyeing their loot. I was surprised at the quantity of money I had. I could not believe I had accumulated that much. I fingered the bills, listened to them rustling, examined the familiar faces of the old gentlemen. I forgot all danger and all caution.

All of a sudden, I heard a squeak. Startled, I froze under the blanket. I heard the door opening. I slid down on the bed very fast, drew the cover up to my chin and lay straight and stiff like a mummy. I saw Father in the door, his dark figure standing out of the white background. He was looking straight at me. I felt the money rustling under me and around me. I tried to look as relaxed and innocent as I could and I even made an unsuccessful effort to smile. Father continued staring at me, strangely serious and immobile. I hoped he would go somewhere, away from my bed. He did not. He must have noticed my fast movements or my frightened eyes, for he looked suspiciously at me and said, "What's the matter with you? What have you got there?" and he started walking towards me in measured steps.

I clung to a last hope. "Nothing, Father, really."

Father stood by my bed. I knew I was lost. I started collecting the bills feverishly under the blanket, trying to sweep them under me. I grabbed a fistful and held it in my burning hand. I remembered God, all of a sudden, and summoned his assistance in a short, frantic prayer. I closed my eyes, hoping Father would not be there when I opened them again. But he was there. Before I could bat an eyelid, he grabbed the edge of my blanket and pulled it off me.

I stared at Father, frightened. His eyes became very big and his pupils got very small. At that moment he too looked frightened. I thought he would start yelling. But he just stepped backwards and leaned against the door of the wardrobe. He squinted and frowned. Beads of sweat appeared on his forehead. Slowly, as in a daze, he walked back towards the bed and gathered a few bills. He kept turning them in his hands in disbelief, then dropped them to the floor. He started pulling the bills from under me and was counting slowly. One hundred . . . two hundred . . . three.

I just lay there immobile for an endless while, feeling cold, then hot, all over, my mind empty of thoughts, watching Father count the bills, moving backwards, moving forwards again, lifting the bills, counting, dropping them on the floor. This was very frightening and I started crying.

Finally Father started talking and his voice sounded strangely hoarse, as if it were coming from somewhere deep within him.

"And what is that?" he said, trying to control the anger that showed in his eyes, and as if he were still hoping for an explanation that would make some sense to him.

I did not answer.

"What is all this money?" he demanded, the note of distress in his voice now clearer.

I stared sobbing loudly.

"Where did you get all this money from? Ah?" He was shaking the headboard of the bed forcefully.

I began crying even louder. "I don't know, Father, I don't know." I did not know which words I should use to tell him.

"But I want to know, and right now!"

He was screaming now and his voice had a shrill, cold tone. I knew I had to tell him now.

"F . . . from pockets, Father, yours and Mother's."

Father stared at me, mute. He placed his hand on his forehead and covered his eyes. He stood like this for a while, immobile, silent. The silence was as difficult for me to bear as his anger. My thoughts were moving tumultuously inside my head, and my head ached as if it could not contain them. Then I saw the door opening slowly, and Mother came in. I knew she offered no salvation, but I looked at her pleadingly. She remained standing at the door, and she watched me accusingly, sternly, waiting for explanations. I shrivelled inside and curled up on my bed. Father took his hand from his eyes. He noticed Mother and waved her away. She left the room. I followed Father's movements anxiously.

He stood there nodding his head for a while, his chin cupped in his hand, his eyes distant, like those of a religious Jew at prayer. Suddenly, for he must have made a decision, his hand moved from his chin to the middle button of his jacket. It stayed there a minute, then slowly, his hand shivering, he unbuttoned the jacket and took it off, all the while looking away from me. Then his hand travelled to the brass buckle of his belt.

I started shivering and opened my eyes wide with fear. My Father was going to belt me! I had never been belted in my life, though Mother sometimes hit me with towels and pillowcases in the past. But my Father . . . Shrivelled and curled into a ball, I retreated to the farthest place on the bed.

I stared at Father with horror. His face was tense and immobile, like a wooden mask. His skin was stretched over his facebones tightly and the stubble on his face looked stiff and sharp, like a thousand dark pins. He undid the belt buckle, then slowly pulled the belt out of the pant hoops.

I closed my eyes. It was so quiet that I could hear Father's heavy breathing and the sound of water gurgling inside the pipes and the distant squeak of a tramway that was turning the corner. I was waiting for the blow to fall and I wished I was on that tramway, going away somewhere.

Suddenly, the safety and the comfort of the darkness was broken by a sharp sound. I heard a crash and the noise of things rattling against each other. I opened my eyes and sat on the bed, startled and scared.

The first thing that I saw was Father's red face. He did not look like my father at all. His eyes were bloodshot, like the eyes of the butcher, Mr. Kugelman, whom we used to know in Russia, and his face was like Mr. Kugelman's too. He was standing looking down at the floor. The realization of what had happened reached me fast.

"No, not my doll house!" I shrieked.

I forgot my fear of Father and, moving towards the edge of my bed, looked down. At my feet was my doll house, all smashed, and in the midst of it was Father's large black shoe.

"No! No! Not my doll house, not my doll house!" I screamed. I grabbed Father's pant leg and tried to pull him away. But Father stepped on the doll house with his foot, again and again, and I could hear how the thin metal walls cracked and collapsed. He looked like an Uzbeck boy I once saw who had destroyed an ant colony. He hit on it again and again, as if he were possessed by an evil spirit, then took a long branch and beat the escaping ants with it. There was a wild, savage look in the boy's eyes.

Father finally stopped, moved away, and his face still red, examined the smashed doll house and me. Then the look in his eyes began changing and became partly angry and partly pained. His lips curved and quivered and his hair was dishevelled and limp. I felt scared and my heart beat painfully and loudly.

Then Mother, alarmed by the noise, appeared in the door. Behind her was Mrs. Lubochinska. They both stared at the wrecked doll house and at me. I was ashamed to face Mrs. Sarah Lubochinska this way and I turned my face to the wall.

"Let's leave her here," I heard Mother addressing Father. "Let her stand here alone and think about what she has done." Mrs. Sarah's deep sigh followed Mother's words.

Father answered her softly. "Please you go out now Mother. I shall stay here with her a while longer."

His soft voice shocked me. He never spoke to Mother in this tone. It was as if they were both ganging up against me in a bond of intimacy. I clenched my fists and I wished I could hit him.

I heard him start talking again, but I just did not listen. Instead, I inched closer to the edge of the bed and looked at the doll house. Malla was lying on her back. Her legs were smashed and her dainty porcelain face was cracked. Next to her lay the Father doll in his little dark suit. He was smashed too. Around them were scattered pieces of the living room broken beyond repair. Everything else was inside.

The sorrow and the pain that welled within me at this sight obliterated all else. My beloved doll house, my little sweet dolls were hurt and smashed. I slipped off the bed and lay crying next to the dolls. I tried to force open the tangled metal walls, but I was too weak, and the metal too hard. So I just lay next to the doll house, put my arms around it and cried bitterly again.

Then I saw Father's shoes and pant legs moving uncertainly, back and forth, around me. He must have just remembered that the doll house was still plugged in, for I saw his hand reach for the plug and pull it out. Then he went to the living room, leaving the door open. After a while I heard Mother, Mrs. Lubochinska and Father's voices. At first they were talking quietly, whispering worried words among themselves, then the voices became loud, more argumentative and strained. Then I heard the door slammed and Mother's high-pitched voice reverberating in the hallway, "Leon, where are you going?"

No sound came in reply.

"Leon, it was just a bunch of toys . . . Leooon!"

I could hear the old wall clock ticking peacefully and I watched its thin arms stretched under the concave shiny glass, the brass pendulum moving sideways rhythmically. The moon, sad and sharp-faced, peeked from between the clouds.

Then I heard the squeak of the iron entrance gate. The sharp points of the bars were scratching the cement pavement. The janitor was locking the yard for the night.

THE CROOKED SMILE

From the moment I arrived in Lodz, two years before, from Russia, where I lived during the war, Polish grammar was for me an unmapped and hostile territory. The long columns of irregular nouns and verbs, which Mrs. Anna Cybulska, my Polish grammar teacher at the Elementary School for Democratic Worker's Children of Lodz, inscribed on the blackboard in her neat, slanted handwriting, were for me ghostly trees in a dark forest, in which I was a small, lost wanderer. Polish nouns are declinable. ...u as such are a source of many complications and much distress in the lives of those who try to master them. I was no exception. So I copied the lists diligently into my notebook and stared at the teacher with sad, uncomprehending eyes.

At home, I spent many hours reciting over and over again, *"Krool, skoora, roozha, plootno,"* which meant "King, leather, rose, cotton." I chanted the words early in the morning, before breakfast, and at night, before going to sleep. I chanted them when playing hopscotch out in the yard. When my friend Halina asked me what it was I was saying, I answered, *"Krool, skoora, roozha, plootno,"* and she knocked with her knuckle on her forehead three times to indicate what she thought of my faculties.

I copied the lists on long strips of paper which, rolled and held in my fist, were to come to my rescue in the event of an unexpected test. The most difficult to remember words and rules I tattoed on the inside of my arm with ink. The arm became gray after a while, for I refused to wash it. The only place where the rules, the verbs and the nouns would not stay was my memory. My brain was immune to grammar.

This, I knew, was bad, for Mrs. Cybulska was very particular when it came to grammar, and this on account of, amoung other things, the deep gratitude she owed it. As she frequently recounted to us, it was grammar that escalated her from the life of toil and misery on a small farm to the position of a teacher in a large industrial town. We often wished she had remained on that small farm.

With this wish in my heart, I stood up beside my desk on that memorable Wednesday afternoon and stared into Mrs. Cybulska's gray eyes. Mrs. Cybulska was dressed in a garb of almost military severity, and a yellowish ivory brooch was pinned above her left breast. She stared at me from beneath her bushy eyebrows and pronounced the words I feared most.

"Decline," she said. "Decline for us the noun 'beginning.'"

In my mind I tried to roll out the long strip of paper. All I could see there was *Krool, skoora, roozha, plootno.* My tattoo was covered by the long sleeve of the tunic and therefore useless. I was lost. *Where did this "beginning" fit? Where was the trick?* I knew Mrs. Cybulska would not ask me to decline a regular noun. I kicked my desk-mate Martha in the ankle. She did not react.

"Beginning, to beginning, of beginning ... " I began, stuttering. A few heads turned towards me, but all I could see in their expressions was how pleased they were it was me standing there stuttering and not them. I made desperate, begging faces at them. But their lips were cruelly pursed. They knew better than to jeopardize themselves on my behalf. And so, my despair went unnoticed and disregarded.

I threw Mrs. Cybulska a look of such utter misery as I thought could dissolve a rock. But she just kept staring at me and shaking her head, as if this was exactly what she had anticipated.

So I did the one thing which I thought could help matters: I smiled. My smile gave me an expression not at all unpleasant and had already accomplished wonders for me with my Math teacher, Mr. Rachyk, a thin man sporting a Chaplinesque moustache. The latter grinned widely whenever I smiled at him and tended to lose all determination to inflict an "F" on me. I had also started noticing that, while my smile did nothing for me with my girl friends, it seemed to affect the boys. Some reddened up to their ears, and their eyes went shifty whenever I smiled at them while asking for an eraser or a blotter to blot the ink stains in my notebook.

I had never tried it on Mrs. Cybulska, for grammar lessons did not inspire me to smile much, but today I thought it was my only hope. I expected to see her stern features melt instantaneously and her face light up in a pleasant way. But a disappointment was lurking for me. Instead of melting, Mrs. Cybulska froze and stiffened, and the brooch above her breast shook. Accentuating her words with slaps to the table top, she said crossly, "Not only have you come to school unprepared, not only you are constantly daydreaming about far-away lands and continents, not only you are missing two buttons on your tunic and allowing your hair to hang in sloppy wisps, but you also have the gall and the daring to make ugly faces at me!"

Mrs. Cybulska was furious, the class was triumphant. They were all laughing like the jackasses that they were, while I stood there, smiling and crying and not knowing what to do.

"But Mrs. Cybulska," I began, shocked and bewildered. My knees started shaking and I felt faint.

"No 'buts' and no 'I's" she interrupted me. She slammed her book closed and added, "Decline fifty nouns in writing for tomorrow. I shall test you after classes. And erase that stupid look from your face!"

I slid into my seat, shaken. I looked around, still hoping to find consolation in the faces of my closer friends, but instead saw in them an odious mixture of spite, glee and mockery. This was a novelty I did not particularly enjoy. As I could not imagine any cause for their mockery, I went over my face with my fingers, suspecting a large wart might have grown there overnight. But my face felt as smooth as a baby's bare buttocks. "Have I got anything on my face?" I whispered to Martha. She looked me over, then shook her head. Mrs. Cybulska observed us from the corners of her gray eyes.

As soon as the bell rang I ran to the washroom. I stared at my face in the mirror. It stared back at me without revealing anything I didn't already know. Mrs. Cybulska was right about the buttons: two were absent from the front of my tunic. I knew that my clothes could do with some tidying, but there was no one in my life who would tidy anything up. My mother was hampered by a university degree which, as she had told Father and me over and over again, she was not going to waste on household chores. Other than that, I saw nothing out of the ordinary. I left the washroom as puzzled and dejected as I had entered it.

When I took my place in the desk, I saw the fat neck of Olek the bald turning and heard him whisper, "Welcome back, Mrs. Quasimodo."

The mention of the hunchback from Notre Dame did not make me more cheerful. With what remained of my spirit I lashed out at Olek, "Be quiet, bald monster!" and considered the conversation, and our relationship, terminated forever.

As soon as classes ended, I rushed out. I wanted to have nothing to do with anyone. All I wanted was a quiet place where I could nurture my grief and my distress undisturbed.

Dragging my feet sadly through side streets and lanes, I arrived at the little park next to St. Boniface's church, not far from where I lived. I was friendly with a few pigeons in that park and it was never too crowded. From the time I had first arrived in Lodz, I had escaped to this park whenever things were becoming difficult for me. Compared to my life in Samarkand, where I lived during the war, life in Lodz seemed gray, dismal and lonely.

I entered the park, swept a few damp leaves off the wooden bench, wiped it dry, and sat down. The park was gray and empty, still wet after the morning rain. The pigeons were indifferent to me; I had no food for them. The park custodian, in a round oilcloth cap and severe uniform, walked around with a metal pick, hunting for papers and candy wraps. There were none, so he just collected a few leaves and threw them carelessly into a garbage bin, then, like an errant comet completing its orbit, he continued circling the paths of the park.

I looked up. The sky, dark gray and streaked with soot and smoke from the many Lodz factory chimneys, gleamed through the trees. The entrance to St. Boniface's church was empty and wind chased the leaves off its stairs. My thoughts went back to Samarkand, where the sky was blue and brilliant and where the landscape of minarets and ancient palaces appeared like a mirage against the desert and the mountains, where blue-bellied swallows dived from the mauve evening sky and where mulberry trees shaded the streets and the noisy vendors of fruits and flowers.

When I returned to Lodz, I hoped to find our old house, my good old Nanny, my aunts and uncles and my grandparents. But the houses were in ruins and the people were dead. The new people I had met here were all strangers and bore sharp-sounding names: Sikorski, Kolski, Sobolevski, so different from the names of Uzbecks in Samarkand, which sounded soft, and meant "Morning Dew" or "Moon Drops" or "Jasmin Flower." People smiled here too, but their smiles were quick and carved deep wrinkles into their faces. The smiles on the faces of Uzbecks were slow and radiant.

It was such a fast life here; everybody seemed to be always busy, coming and going and laughing nervously. My parents, too, were like large birds, constantly flapping their wings and rushing about, unable to take off in any direction; like these pigeons that kept hopping around the garbage bins. Mother worked, Father worked, maids came and left with much noise about the wages and stolen things, guests came frequently to the house, ate, drank, some returned a few times, others did not.

On my way home from the park I saw Mr. Kuba's grocery store. Mr. Kuba's store was famous for the variety and the quality of its candies and I knew that a few "Soft Cows," caramel candies filled with fudge, were just the thing to make my life more bearable. I also hoped for the consoling sight of jovial Mr. Kuba, an old and trusted friend, into whose pockets went all my allowance.

Mr. Kuba was standing under an obituary-like sign that proclaimed "Credit is Dead," with a bored expression on his face. He was busily scratching the bald spot on his head, while a fly circled noisily above it. Behind him stood jars with candies, nuts and chocolates. I smiled at him and waited for a smile to appear on his face. Instead, his face underwent a sudden metamorphosis of astonishment and concern. He turned away from me, shook his head as if he had swallowed something bitter, and spat into a spittoon which he kept behind the counter. I hoped he was well and voiced my concern. He said he was well. I said I was well too and asked for a few "Cows." He handed them to me with greater than usually alacrity and without the pleasant cordiality that I was accustomed to. Then he surprised me by refusing to accept payment, telling me it was a small matter, indeed, and why didn't I go home and take a rest.

I did not feel I needed rest, and told him so. His manner was so unusual and so disturbing that I rushed up the stairs without even thanking him. I was also afraid lest he change his mind about the payment. Sucking on a Soft Cow I entered the yard of the apartment complex where we lived.

Looking at that yard was not something that I listed among pleasures, for it was a very sorry piece of real estate. Shaped like a long triangle, it was paved with gray, lumpy cement. It smelled of cooked cabbage and mildew. The buildings that surrounded it were a dirty yellowish colour and looked as if many generations of housewives had poured laundry water down their walls. At the yard's end stood a small outhouse, which did nothing to make the appearance or the smell of the place more pleasant, and the few flowers that were planted around it looked as if they had emerged out of the seed already wilted.

I crossed the yard and entered door number four. We lived on the second floor, in apartment number eight. As I climbed the dim stairs I thought about how almost everything here was measured and numbered. In Samarkand I hardly noticed numbers. One bought sunflower seeds by the glass, vegetables and fruits by the piece or by the bunch, other things by the bag. Lengths were measured by the distance between the thumb and the pinky of outstretched fingers, or by the distance from the fist to the elbow. The streets in Samarkand were short and only a few of the houses had numbers.

I reached the door of the apartment, lifted the mat, and took out a key that was hidden underneath, then I opened the heavy door and stepped in. The familiar smell of gefilteh fish announced to me that our tenant, Mrs. Sarah Lubochinska, was at home and that she was cooking her Friday meal, probably in eager anticipation of the visit of her daughter Sabena's principal suitor, the fat Joseph Leviathan. Joseph Leviathan was very partial to Mrs. Sarah's culinary talents.

Mrs. Sarah and her daughter moved into the third, small room of our apartment shortly after our cousins Eva and Sol left for Paris. They were assigned to us by the lodging committee of the town of Lodz and they filled our kitchen with an assortment of pots and pans of every size, shape and description. My mother was not happy with this invasion. She said that the tenants were going to crowd us out of the kitchen. Why she was so concerned I could not understand, for she seldom entered there. She also complained that Mrs. Lubochinska was "common" and "uneducated." But my father took one look at Sabena who was a statuesque brunette with red lips, and he voiced no objection whatsoever to their tenancy.

I myself was quite excited about having the two move in with us. From the time Mother started working, the apartment had been empty when I came home from school, and I did not like coming home to an empty apartment. I spent much of my free time in the company of my cat, which was fine if one enjoyed monologues.

After Sarah and Sabena Lubochinska moved in, things became more pleasant for me. Mrs. Sarah was always in the kitchen, the apartment smelled of good food, which she sometimes gave me to taste, and our front door rang frequently to announce the arrival of another one of Sabena's many suitors. I took great interest in them and expressed my opinions freely and honestly, which was not always to Sabena's liking. She did not like, for example, when I referred to Joseph Leviathan as "fat." But that was what he was and I found no reason for calling him anything else. Sabena said he was "well built" and "manly," but that was her opinion.

I took off my coat and pushed the kitchen door open. Mrs. Lubochinska was at her post by the stove, holding a ladle in her hand and peeping into a steaming pot. She was wrapped in a shiny, black kimono-style robe, which was embroidered with birds and butterflies in flight and in repose. Two of the butterflies perched on Mrs. Sarah's breasts. They looked lost and forlorn there, for her breasts were large enough to accommodate a whole swarm of butterflies. The rest of her body was small by comparison and full of fatty folds and double chins, for Mrs. Lubochinska liked not only to cook, but also to eat what she had cooked.

"Good day, Mrs. Sarah, what's cooking today?" I addressed her amiably and smiling, hoping to be treated to whatever she had in that delicious-smelling pot. The hope vanished as soon as her face emerged from behind the vapours and she had a good look at me.

"What's the matter with you, child?" she said. "You can't keep a straight face anymore?"

I told her I did not want to keep a straight face, that I wanted to smile at her and that was what I did.

"Oh, so you have done it on purpose? Shame on you to do things like these to your old friend, Mrs. Sarah!"

I wanted to tell her I did not intend to do anything disrespectful, that I was not laughing at her, but she had no time or patience to listen to me.

"All right, all right, child," she said impatiently. "We'll discuss it later. I'm busy now, as you see, for Mr. Leviathan will be coming for dinner!" The felicity of this prospect caused her small features to expand in a wide, radiant smile, but it lasted a short moment only. She scowled as she glanced at me again, then added, "Now go to your room and take a rest."

She was the second person who had urged me to rest and third to be unpleasant to me. I was bewildered, for I felt no different from before. I reminded myself that adults acted strangely sometimes, and that on those occasions one was supposed to keep quiet and not to ask too many questions. My mother called it "nerves." So I figured that they all were afflicted with a case of "nerves." I gave Mrs. Sarah a sad look and quietly withdrew from the kitchen.

For consolation I turned to the cat, who purred peacefully on my bed. I sank my face into his soft, furry belly and held him tightly. But he too became impatient after a while and wriggled out of my embrace. I sat at my desk to decline the fifty accursed nouns.

Around six o'clock my mother appeared in the door. I could tell she must have had a chat with Mrs. Lubochinska, for she looked at me suspiciously and watchfully. My mother's face always looked as if she expected the worst to happen to her any minute. She told me that life had supplied her with enough reasons for that, myself being not the least. For lack of convincing evidence to the contrary I believed her. So I stared at that face of hers and although I had no particularly strong reasons to smile at her, I did.

What happened then was much more dramatic than anything that had occurred during the earlier hours of that unpleasant day. My mother clutched her bosom with both hands and cried "No!" in such a heartbreaking way that I stopped smiling, sprang from the chair and ran to the medicine cabinet to fetch her valerian drops.

When I returned to the bedroom carrying the lifesaving drops in my hand, my mother seemed to have recovered. She just sat there staring at me fixedly, then yelled, "What is that? What is it, tell me?"

I ran to the mirror and stared at myself again but, seeing nothing out of the ordinary, turned to Mother.

"What is what, Mother? Why is everyone staring at me as if I were a monster? I cannot understand! I see nothing wrong!"

Mother had recovered enough strength to rise to her feet, grab me from behind by my shoulders and push me to the oval mirror of the bedroom cupboard.

"Smile!" she ordered.

I did not feel like smiling then and there, but my mother was not a person one dared to disobey. So I stood in front of the mirror and I smiled at myself. And I gasped, and I covered my lips with my hand right away. Everything that had happened to me on that day became all at once understandable to me, for what I saw on my face was a grimace of indescribable ugliness.

My mother stood behind me, looking the way Lot's wife must have looked after her last glance at Sodom. Her eyes were sorrowful and her cheeks fallen. Her second chin formed a fold beneath her face, as if to keep her face from collapsing. She wove her fingers into a gesture of despair

136

"We are going to become the laughing stock of the whole town," she said.

I did not care about the opinion of the town of Lodz and the verdict it might proclaim upon me, but my face was an entirely different matter and a cause of deep concern. I removed my hand from my mouth, and I dared to smile at myself again. It looked as if someone had attached to my lips two pulleys, which were set into motion by a delinquent nerve in my brain. The lower lip was pulled down on the left side, while the upper arched up in the same corner, exposing to the world two of my teeth. I remembered Olek the Bald's reference to Quasimodo and had to admit that it was not entirely out of place. The initial shock of this revelation left me speechless. Then I started crying. Still crying, I inserted my two index fingers into the corners of my mouth and tried to stretch it. This hurt, but accomplished nothing. Frustrated, angry and sad, I sat on the floor and hid my face in my hands.

To confound things even more the door-bell rang and Mother went out. Soon after, I heard the pleasant, warm voice of Uncle Sternfeld, a jovial friend of the family and by common consent of all who knew him, a "homely sage" who frequently dropped in for tea. He rolled his ample frame through my door, almost pushed from behind by Mother. She must have briefed him about my condition, for he approached me carefully, as if I would bite. He had round, bulging eyes, which gave him the expression of a French bulldog, and which frequently scrutinized my budding breasts quite voluptuously. His fingers were so plump that, had they been made of fabric, they could have easily served as pincushions.

Carefully, he sat on the bed and took me by the wrist as if he were going to check my pulse. He exuded an aura of well-being and the scent of mild but good cologne, and looked like a person who had just finished consuming an excellent meal in a first-class restaurant. Through my tears, I smiled at him.

Although he was forewarned, he was not prepared. He stared at me as if I were afflicted with leprosy. Then he exclaimed, "My poor, poor child, whatever happened to your pretty smile?" and he kissed me and wiped the tears off my face with his embroidered handkerchief. He then got up, took Mother by the elbow and they both advanced towards the living room where, I was sure, they were going to conduct a hurried conference above tea with biscuits.

I returned to stare at myself in the mirror. I tried the stretching act again, but with similar results. Mother's and Uncle Sternfeld's voices reached me from the living room, one shrill and loud, the other calm and reassuring.

The days that followed were, compared to the one that preceded them, quiet and serene. I avoided unpleasantness by keeping a straight face. My unsmiling self did not cause any stir at school. Only Martha inquired whether I had had any funerals in my family lately. I replied that apart from the demise of a few mice in the paws of my cat, there were no unexpected deaths around me. Mrs. Cybulska tested me orally again, was quite pleased with my progress and declared that there was some hope for me after all.

My father had been on an out-of-town assignment and so had been spared the sight of me. Mrs. Lubochinska, as if to compensate for her initial unkindness, pulled me to her bosom frequently, said, "My poor child!" and spoiled me with dollops of mashed potatoes with butter and dill or with broiled breasts of chicken in garlic. My mother avoided the subject of my deformity.

For a while, things were quiet and nobody did anything to shatter the equilibrium. But one day, about a week after the discovery, there was a surprise waiting for me when I arrived from school. The living room was brightly illuminated, as for a holiday, and the table was covered with a white tablecloth. Our good china was taken out of the credenza. At the table were Mrs. Sarah Lubochinska, Uncle Sternfeld, Mother and Father, who must have arrived back in town that morning, earlier than anticipated. The four had the expressions of well-fed hawks about to savour a small morsel of tender meat for dessert. Mother's and Mrs. Lubochinska's breasts rested on the table, as if the inferior-quality postwar corsets were unable to give them the proper support. Both must have paid an afternoon visit to a beauty parlour, for their hair was rolled into very small, then-fashionable curls, and their eyebrows were plucked into thin lines, which gave their faces slightly puzzled expressions.

138

Father was sitting at the head of the table. He looked uncomfortably serious. When I entered, his lips started quivering. One glance from Mother, and they were not quivering any more. They all looked so tense and behaved in such an unnatural way, that I lost my resolve and smiled.

This had an electrifying effect on the assembled. My mother hid her face in her hands, while Mrs. Lubochinska clutched her breast at the spot, where, deep down, beat her kind and vulnerable heart. Only Uncle Sternfeld twiddled his plump thumbs calmly, as he smiled back at me.

I observed the scene, bemused and mute. Father was speechless. Mother uncovered her face, stared at him tensely, then stretched her arm towards him and sank her freshly manicured fingernails into the shoulder-cushions of his jacket.

"Tell me!" she yelled at him. "Tell me what should be done? Lose your composure once in a lifetime! Can't you see? Your only daughter, the great grand-daughter of the venerable head of the city of Ozorkov, and a grand-daughter of your own Father, a distinguished owner of the tallest chimney in the city of Lodz, may they rest in peace, looks like a freak, a degenerate, a blemish, and you are calm and composed? Say something, do something, for God's sake!"

Mrs. Lubochinska gave Father a long and reproachful look. My father, who was not a big man, seemed to have shrunk. He stared at me as if I were a present he had just received and did not know what to do with. But the mention of his venerable forefathers must have had its impact upon him, for he got up from his chair, cleared his throat and made an impressive gesture with his hand, as if he was preparing to make a momentous announcement.

Everybody stared at him hopefully.

But he sat down as quickly as he got up and shook his head, as if admitting defeat. Mother leaned her forehead on her hand, in a gesture that was intended to communicate utter despair, and Mrs. Sarah moved her breasts from the table and heavily leaned back against her chair.

Silence reigned in the room for a while. A deep frown appeared on Father's forehead, then he moved his shoulders, as if determined to shake off the ancestors that sat perched there.

"I admit that our family had its share of deformities and afflictions ... " he said. "We had a hunchback and two cousins with deformed noses. Then there was, if my memory serves me well, 'Wolf the Blind,' 'Rivkeh the Toothless,' and 'Itsek the Meshuggeh.' But ... " Here he raised himself from his chair, and announced decisively and finally, "But we had no crooked smiles!" He hit the table with his fists and his eyes rested on Mother, as if he were thus relegating all responsibility for my condition to her side of the genealogical tree.

But Mother would have none of this. She just stared at him with an expression of contempt and with eyes that asked, "How dare you?"

"We were the aristocracy of the region," she said proudly. "Our women were known for their beauty and intelligence. *We* had no hunchbacks and no cousins with deformed limbs. What we did have, however, were some perfect beauties, famous in the region of Bialystock."

Mrs. Lubochinska, who held Mother's university degree in awe and in great esteem, nodded forcefully. I glanced at Mother doubtfully, searching for traces of the perfection that she had mentioned. Though she was not bad looking, considering wear and tear, the war and other factors, perfection was rather hard to find.

My parents, having thus relieved their ancestors of responsibility stared at each other like two roosters about to start a fight. I was sure they would have exchanged a few more pleasantries if it were not for the presence of strangers. Instead, they directed their half-worried and half-accusing glances at me. But I just stood there and pulled at the tail of the cat, secretly enjoying the commotion I had caused. The advantages that were coming my way because of that crooked smile were becoming obvious to me and the feeling that went with this thought was not at all unpleasant.

Mrs. Lubochinska, who until then had kept in the background, must have felt that her turn to enter the scene had arrived.

"Who, tell me, would want to marry a girl with a crooked smile, I am asking?" she said. "My Sabena, may the Almighty be thanked and spare us further sorrows, does not have anything crooked, and yet we have problems in the question of marriage. I am afraid, Mr. Leon, that you will have to start thinking about a considerable dowry to compensate the future groom for the defect."

The idea seemed to amuse Father. His thoughts had never dwelled on dowries, neither then nor when he had married my mother. This only strenghthened the mild contempt that his immediate family had for his impracticality and honesty. Everybody had predicted that these qualities would warrant him at best a genteel level of poverty, and he did not disappoint them.

"If this is the main concern, we shall have to do something about it before she reaches the marrying age!" Father said decisively. Then, considering the conference adjourned, he got up, pinched me on the cheek and told me not to worry, that he was going to think about a solution. Though I had no great confidence in my father's ability to perform miracles, I was pleased he took the thing lightly. I felt free to depart and let the four of them have their well-deserved cup of tea.

A few days later my parents announced that I would not be going to school the following morning. They also presented me with a new pleated skirt and a white blouse with a round, lace collar. They did not explain their sudden generosity, but I knew it had something to do with my smile. Perhaps with my face thus disfigured, they wanted to decorate the rest of me. I was ready to hold on to that smile indefinitely, or at least until I was equipped with a decent wardrobe.

The next morning my parents composed a letter of apology to my teachers, citing a "sudden mild illness" as the cause for my absence. Although it was a Tuesday, they put on their Sunday best and new dark coats. They spent the entire morning rushing about, making telephone calls, conferring in the corridor with Mrs. Lubochinska and with Sabena. With solemn and secretive expressions they urged me to wash thoroughly and not to forget the nape of my neck and the inside of my ears. It was like preparing for Passover, but holiday time was too distant for me to consider it the reason for all this excitement. I tried to question my parents, but their replies were noncommital and vague.

Around eleven o'clock we went down the stairs and out into the street, all three of us festive looking. At the corner a buggy was waiting for passengers, and we climbed in solemnly. With protective gestures, my parents seated me in the middle. It was as if all of a sudden I had acquired added value for them. And so, one crooked smile was doing what years of proper behaviour, neat notebooks and good marks failed to accomplish: I was getting new clothes, my parents were taking a day off for me and I was driven by a buggy to some mysterious place. And so, although I could not smile at the world, the world was beginning to smile at me.

The buggy-man asked Father for directions and cried *"Vio!"* to his horse, which looked as if it were quite ready to spend the rest of the afternoon munching its groats on that street corner. A few more *"Vio!"*'s and a few pulls on the reins finally convinced the horse to start. The street was paved with round stones, which were called "cats' heads" and we proceeded on their uneven surface with jolts, jerks and twists. The black canopy of the buggy shook and shivered, and I giggled with every jolt. My parents were mortified, but restrained themselves from slapping me or even from uttering a remark. They must have decided to play it safe. Luckily for them it started drizzling and the driver opened the folding roof over our heads, which spared them further embarrassment.

About half an hour later the buggy stopped on a narrow street, in front of a house designated by number 18. It was a handsome old building, with an intricately carved façade and wide, clean windows. There was a sign near the entrance— black letters on white enamel—which said "Dr. Sheinzon, Child Psychiatrist and Neurologist." Although I was not familiar with some of the words that appeared on the sign, something told me it was there we were headed. I understood now the reason for my parents' evasiveness, the new clothes and the morning scrubbing. I pulled angrily at Father's sleeve.

"Is this where we are going?" I pointed to the sign.

"Yes," he answered curtly, as if it were a daily habit of ours to ride a buggy to doctors' offices.

"And what for, Father?"

I knew. I just wanted to hear it from him.

"For your crooked smile."

"Ay, ay!" I yelled. "You shameless schemers! You have bribed and tricked me into it. It's not fair! I am not going!"

My parents stared at me, and at each other, helplessly. They knew I had a stubborn and rebellious streak in me, but it had never manifested itself so violently, and out in the open air. So they just stood above me, resembling, in their dark long coats, two large penguins. My mother appeared quite ready to resort to the use of her right hand, but Father restrained her. I stared at him then, and Father looked so forlorn and miserable, that I decided to do it for him. I would go see Dr. Sheinzon.

Walking heavily we climbed the stairs. Mother was nervous, Father was calm, but held me by the hand, as if to avert any attempt at escape. On the first floor of the building was a language school and on the second I noticed a handwritten sign that said "Hebrew Youth Organization." I did not know what "Hebrew" meant, but this was not the time to inquire. Dr. Sheinzon's office was on the third floor. My mother pressed the bell button with determination and stood in front of it, panting. I was angry, curious and impatient. I hoped we were too early or too late, or that the doctor had been called away.

After a while, I heard the sounds of heavy steps coming from behind the door, and someone's merry whistling. Then the door opened and I saw the doctor standing there, all six feet of him. I eyed him distrustfully. But then I had a good look at him and my mistrust vanished, for his face was full of folds, like that of a St. Bernard, and he had the kindest pair of gray eyes, which looked at me moistly, as if I were the first little girl he had ever seen. Then he put his hand out in greeting to me, as if I were an adult. I extracted my hand from Father's clutch, and placed it in the doctor's big paw. Then I smiled at him. At that moment something quite unexpected happened. The doctor squatted, like a small boy, so that his face was at the level of mine, and he smiled back at me. And lo and behold! The doctor sported a crooked smile.

This was something I was totally unprepared for and, at first, I was confused and did not know how to react. So I just went on smiling. And so, the doctor and I kept staring at each other like two mischievous buddies who had met in the street. Then we both burst out laughing and kept at it for a while, totally oblivious to my parents, who stood above me like two columns, much less jolly than the doctor and I, and quite obviously disoriented by this turn of events.

"So, we are birds of a feather," the doctor said amicably and I nodded at him. He must have noticed my parents' confusion, for he said, very quickly, "The cause, though, may not be quite the same. I suffered from a disease as a child. But these things happen for a variety of reasons . . ." And he glanced briefly at my mother. Then he rose to his full height and, hovering protectively above my parents, explained to them that because of his own problem he had researched the subject thoroughly. This speech seemed to calm them, and we all proceeded to the waiting room, where he asked them to wait.

Then he took me to his cabinet, which was unlike any doctor's office I had ever seen and which looked more like my school principal's office. To my surprise the doctor did not ask me to undress but, instead, pulled up a chair for me and asked me, very kindly, to sit there.

Then he asked whether I knew that a few very prominent people had crooked smiles, and among them was a famous king of Poland, who even in history books appeared as Boleslav the Crooked-Mouthed. Yes, I knew about this king and have seen his picture. I smiled again, for I realized that in addition to all other benefits, I was also in good company. Then the doctor handed a book to me and asked me to read a paragraph. It was a paragraph about this very king, but it did not dwell upon his affliction, instead concentrating on the fact that he had caused the division of Poland in the eleventh century or so. When I finished reading the paragraph, the doctor said that I read clearly and intelligently. It felt good to be praised. Then he asked me to write a short composition for him and I wrote a description of Sabena and Sarah Lubochinska and of Sabena's principal suitor, Joseph Leviathan, merchant in jewels, and I told how Sabena's eyes sparkled whenever he appeared, wiggling his fat pinky, to the tip of which was attached a very small box. I described how I peeped into their room through the keyhole, and what I saw there, and how they had once noticed my blue eye there and had put a wad of cotton in the hole.

Dr. Sheinzon read my story with a huge crooked grin on his face and sometimes he laughed loudly. This in turn made me giggle and in the end the two of us once again sat across from each other laughing heartily. I laughed even louder when it occurred to me what fun the two of us were having while my parents were sitting in the corridor like two sad hens.

Dr. Sheinzon became serious then and he questioned me about my school and my friends and how I was getting along with them. I told him about Bald Olek and he smiled again. Then he asked about my parents and that was where we both stopped laughing, for at some moments I felt like crying and the doctor looked at me with concern. I was surprised at myself telling him all these things, for I had always kept them to myself. I was ashamed to tell anyone who was not close to me, and there were no close people around: just tenants and acquaintances. The doctor cracked a small joke, and I smiled through tears. He also said he was going to ask my parents to send me over again, and I was pleased and thankful to him.

Before I left I reminded him that we had not discussed the crooked smile at all. His face had a wistful look when he answered that I should not worry about it, that it was going to disappear one day, without any effort or intervention on my part. This sounded unbelievable, but reassuring, and I went out much more confident and happy than when I came in.

Then the doctor invited my parents in. They stayed in the doctor's cabinet a long while. I sat in the waiting room wondering whether the doctor had asked them to write a composition too. When they finally emerged, they looked like two children who had been harshly reprimanded by the school principal. Their eyes became shifty when they looked at me, and Mother kept repeating to herself, "Such nonsense, such nonsense, who's ever heard such nonsense as this." But it was clear to me she was not at ease with herself. Father stared at her with an expression that said, "It's all your fault, you see," and she answered him with a look that said, "No, it's yours."

We took a buggy again, and all the way back my mother and father were quiet. Both kept looking out into the street. I was serene and felt important. My chest was warm and comfortable. When we got home Father helped me to take my coat off and he hung it on the hook in the corridor, a thing I could not remember him doing from the time I was small. Mrs. Lubochinska was waiting for us anxiously. She exchanged glances full of concern with my parents and became more cheerful only after they had indicated with gestures of their hands that things were under control. She then took me to the kitchen, where a plate of potato dumplings richly smothered with onions was waiting for me.

I started visiting Dr. Sheinzon's office regularly, every Tuesday afternoon after school. He was more like a teacher than a doctor. He never examined my chest or ears and instead engaged me in conversation, which was not a problem for me, for I had inherited from my mother an innate and immoderate ability to use words.

Some of the things he was telling me, though, were at first very strange and frightening, for they were totally contrary to my mother's teachings. Her golden rule, which she had hammered into me since infancy was "Fish and Children Have No Voice." The doctor told me this was not so, and that I should answer her back. I knew that this activity might be followed by a slap, so I went about it carefully and hesitantly. When, however, I did dare to answer her back once, no slap came. She remained speechless and tightlipped and frowning. She did recover her speech after a while, but what she said was mild and weak.

Then the doctor said that I could do with some decent things to wear. I told him I knew that I lacked nice clothes, but was afraid to ask for them, for my parents constantly quarrelled about money and complained that they did not have any to spare. What the doctor said then shocked and pleased me at the same time: he told me not to believe everything my parents and other people said. Surprised, I asked whether he thought my parents were liars. He only smiled in reply, and I understood. This made me feel quite good; I was not the only liar in the family. My parents were untruthful too and not at all the towers of virtue that I though they were. This realization had the strange effect of making me like them better.

That same evening I positioned myself across from Mother at the living room table, and with a conspirator's smile made my request. She stiffened in an attempt to demonstrate to me that

146

under the circumstances what I was asking for was inconsiderate and outrageous. Then I said, "Dr. Sheinzon said you could well afford it!" She pulled the long, surprised face of an indignant queen, then faked a small heart seizure. She recovered quite quickly and without the aid of valerian drops, and said she was going to discuss it with Father, as if Father had a say in any matter in our house.

The outcome of this conference (if it ever took place) must have been positive, for a few days later Mother escorted me to the building where her own exclusive dressmaker, Mrs. Eveleena Levandovska, occupied an apartment in a house with an elevator. She received us with a regal mien, and after brief but heated negotiations agreed to sew a dress for me.

On my way up to Dr. Sheinzon's office I always heard the noise of animated voices coming from behind the doors of the Hebrew Youth Organization quarters. It had never occurred to me I could just go in. It was the doctor who suggested that I should. Because of my smile I was reluctant, but he urged me to try.

I knocked on the door one day and stood waiting, listening to the noise. A girl my age finally opened the door and smiled. She told me her name was Tsipora or Tsipa, and that in Hebrew it meant "a bird." She did not look like a bird, though; with her mature freckled face, sharp brown eyes and a well-developed bust she looked like a small adult. I, with my round collar, braids and ribbons felt like a child. But she reassured me in a warm voice, speaking Polish with a heavy Yiddish inflection. She encouraged me to follow her into the large room at the end of the corridor.

The activity had already begun when we entered. A young suntanned man with curly black hair and flaming eyes was addressing a group of youngsters who reclined on old sofas, sat on the floor and window sills or leaned against the walls. Some of the kids smoked cigarettes. Girls had their arms entwined inside the arms and around the shoulders of boys. I felt like a small chick suddenly introduced into the company of hens and roosters. I was overcome with shyness and wanted to withdraw, but Tsipa pulled on my hand and made me sit next to her, on the floor.

The young man spoke with great vigor about the sufferings of Jews throughout the centuries. He said there must be an end to these sufferings and the humiliations. He said that there was hope now, for the first time in millenia and that we should feel privileged and honored to be living at such a time. He then said the words *"Erets Israel,"* the land of Israel. These words, which I was hearing for the first time, imprinted a warm feeling in my heart. It was as if I had always known the words deep within me, and the memory was surfacing now. The young man had just come from the Land of Israel, and he spoke about the country using words similar to the ones I used when I talked of or thought about Samarkand. He described its long sandy beaches, blue skies and warm weather all year long. He spoke of the brilliant sunsets, the palm trees and the minarets, and about people who were kind and helpful and who wanted to share things with each other. I could see that land before me as if I had been there long long ago.

At the end of the "activity" some of the kids surrounded the young man, and others surrounded me. They asked me many questions, and when they heard I came from Samarkand, they became curious and asked me to sit in the middle and tell them all about it. I was shy at first and afraid I would mumble and stutter, but their proddings were so sincere that in the end I relented and sat, crosslegged, in the middle of the room and I described to them some of what I knew and remembered of this beautiful and ancient city, where Shehrezade had once lived. They listened to me as avidly as they had listened to the young man with curly hair and the flaming eyes. I was thrilled and I promised I would come again.

I went home prancing and humming to myself a tune I had just learned in Hebrew, even though I did not understand the words. It was as if a whole new world had suddenly opened before me, and suddenly I felt free as a bird. These kids were so different from the polite kids in my school in their ironed jackets and stiff ties. I was one of them. When I came home I told Mrs. Lubochinska about the "activity" and she was happy and clapped her hands. My parents were less enthusiastic, but they agreed that I could continue going there.

From then on, after every visit to Dr. Sheinzon's office, I went down to the second floor. A boy named Shloymo started sitting next to me wherever I sat. One day he offered to take me home. I would have liked it more if another boy, who resembled my childhood friend Samenchuk had asked me instead, but he did not and Shloymo did and it was getting late and dark outside.

This Shloymo had a funny habit of addressing everyone, "Hey you!" and this habit irritated me. But he had his good points. He was a year and a half older than I, and I felt flattered that a person so tall and so mature should take an interest in me. He also did not have any pimples and freckles on his face and neck, the way the boys in my class did, and he did not resemble in the least Olek the Bald. He did have, however, the beginning of a thin growth above his lip, which I at first mistook for dirt.

He offered to take me home after the next activity too and after the one that followed. He always had some pressing business in my part of town. Once it was a dying aunt, another time it was a small cousin who needed help with homework. He did not appear to be in a great rush to reach them, however, for we always walked instead of riding the tramway, and then stood in front of my house till it became dark. We had plenty to talk about. We discussed the activities, books and people we knew, talked about politics and changes, our schools and teachers. After a while I noticed that talking to him was somewhat different from talking to other people, and I sometimes wished we could remain together longer.

After a while he did not need any more excuses, for I stood waiting for him at the door at the end of every activity. I noticed that he was not bad looking at all, in spite of his glasses, which had earned him the nickname "intelligentsia" and in spite of his longish nose. He had nice wavy hair, a dark complexion and very dark eyes which looked at me moistly too. He hid with the partisans, in the forest, during the war and he had no parents. He lived with his uncle, who had found him after the war. He read a lot and knew many things, and was someone a person could talk to, as I explained to Dr. Sheinzon, who welcomed Shloymo's appearance with a wink and a smile.

One evening, as we were entering the dim vestibule of our apartment building, Shloymo said, "Hey you, you are a pretty and intelligent girl and everything, but how come you are always so serious. Haven't they taught you at home how to smile, or are you in mourning?"

I leaned against the wall and reluctantly confided my secret to him. In the dim light I saw his face lighting up in an impish smile. He was breathing faster than usual when he said, "I have a secret to tell you, you know. I happen to be a famous magician in disguise and I specialize in the cure of the very affliction from which you suffer, my dear." Then, before I had even the chance to cry "Hey you!" he stooped above me, held my hands down and pressed his lips against mine. Then he was kissing me so fast I could hardly breathe. I tried to fight him off, but his hands held mine strongly. I tried to kick, but he pressed his legs against mine and suddenly I found myself flattened between Shloymo and the wall. It was not such a bad feeling, so after a while I stopped objecting so violently. He then let me go and asked me to kiss him, but the shreds of self-respect that dangled limply inside me commanded me to resist, and I refused.

We continued curing my smile this way after every activity. Once Shloymo told me that the cure might be more complete if he put his hand on my breast and he proceeded without procuring my consent. But I did not object strongly, for by then I believed him; he was known as a very honest boy.

Once we surprised Sabena and Joseph Leviathan occupying "our" wall. They got scared and rushed upstairs, leaving the field, or rather the wall, to us.

At the end of that year Sabena got engaged to Joseph Leviathan, to the great satisfaction of Mrs. Lubochinska. The wedding party, for which Mrs. Lubochinska cooked and baked for two weeks and prepared mountains of food took place in our living room, around the oval mahogany table and under the fully-lit chandelier. It was a festive occasion indeed. There were eight of us at the table: Sabena and Joseph, Mother and Father, Uncle Sternfeld, Mrs. Sarah, Shloymo and myself. Shloymo came wearing a suit and looking very mature. He brought two bonbonnieres and two bouquets of flowers, for Sabena and for me. We all ate and drank. Mother was in an unusually good mood, and even told a few spicy jokes, which made the engaged couple blush. Father got slightly drunk, pinched the fiancée on the buttocks and kissed her more times than my mother considered proper. She expressed her opinion aloud and Father retorted, "Is it a wedding or isn't it?" and went on. Mrs. Sarah cast coquettish glances in the direction of Uncle Sternfeld, who did not remain indifferent and caressed her plump elbow every time she brought him a dish with food. I wore a new silk dress sewn by Mrs. Eveleena Levandovska in person. I too drank wine and was mildly intoxicated when I recited the poem which I had composed in honour of the occasion.

In the poem I praised Mrs. Sarah's culinary efforts on our behalf, lauded Mr. Leviathan and the persistence of his courtship, said how sorry we would all be to lose Sabena, but added that her happiness was going to be our consolation and wished the newlyweds many radiant smiles on the many miles of their life together. I ended with the hope that we would all meet again in the land of Israel.

I was cheered and applauded by everyone and all the guests kissed me in turn. Shloymo kissed me on both cheeks and became all flushed. Mr. Leviathan bought the poem from me and paid me 500 zloty, which was a small fortune and the largest honorarium I had ever received. He hid the poem in the left pocket of his jacket, "close to the heart and the wallet," as he said. My parents beamed proudly and patted me on the back and Mother mumbled something about apples that do not fall far from trees.

Then Joseph Leviathan put a record on the gramophone and we all danced the tango. Father danced with Sabena, who was taller than he and his face bumped against her breasts, which he did not seem to mind. Joseph Leviathan danced with Mother and was very gallant to her, which made her smile contentedly. Mrs. Sarah snuggled against Uncle Sternfeld in a way that made me suspect that she harbored some plans regarding him in her mind. Shloymo and I did not know how to dance the tango, so we just shuffled our feet, bumped into each other and giggled.

It was too crowded in the living room, so we moved to the bedroom and tried to practice the tango there. We stopped in front of the oval mirror and I stared at myself, startled how different I looked in my new dress of pale green silk with pink rosebuds, my hair falling to my shoulders in waves, my cheeks blushed and my lips red and full. My breasts were round and firm. When I smiled, the corners of my lips curled up evenly; my smile was new and untroubled. The crooked smile was but a memory now.

The sound of glasses clinking against each other came from the living room. Then I heard the sound of glass being crushed; the bridegroom was breaking the traditional glass by stamping on it with his foot. A chorus of congratulations followed. Shloymo went to the living room to congratulate the newlyweds and I remained alone. I approached the window, and looked out into the yard. The air was suffused with the smell of jasmine and the yard was softly dark. My thoughts went back a year and I remembered Mrs. Cybulska and the oral exam in the declension of nouns. I could decline nouns well now. I began silently, "Beginning, to beginning, of beginning..." and I continued until I heard Shloymo's steps behind me.